SHE

Ma

Text copyright ©2014 Maxine Ebdon
All Rights Reserved

To Jayne, for showing me that through determination and despite hardship anything can be achieved.

Table of Contents

Chapter 1

It was Saturday morning; weekends were always the worst. Mandy ran out of the kitchen door to the back garden, tears rolling down her tiny face. She didn't mean to knock her drink over, but her hands were shaking so much that she just couldn't hold the cup steady.

As she reached the shed at the back of the garden she heard the sound of glass shattering. Mum had taken her rage out on the kitchen wall and thrown the empty bottle at it, storming back up the stairs to bed, cursing as she went.

The shed had become a welcome place for little Mandy; it was the one place where she was relatively safe. It's hard to imagine how life had changed in the past two years. Mummy hardly ventured outside to the garden now; it used to be one of the best kept gardens in the neighbourhood; with meticulously planned borders, a vegetable patch, even a play area with a slide and swing for Mandy to play on. There was a large greenhouse where Ruby would work for hours, planting seeds and taking cuttings for her friends and neighbours. Sunflowers were Mandy's favourite- they would grow so high! She would place them in pots at the back of the garden, next to the shed. Sometimes Ruby would make a picnic and they would spend hours in the garden together.

These were good times. Every day was a good day. Ruby would do everything possible to make sure that Mandy was happy. They went on trips to the park, the zoo and the beach; and when Mandy's father Derek had his annual holiday from work they would drive down to Devon for two weeks.

Mandy didn't see a lot of her father; he worked in the North Sea on an oilrig. He was away for months at a time and then only home for a few weeks. Time would go so fast when he was home! The first couple of days Derek would spend catching up on sleep and then Viv and Joyce, Derek's parents would come for dinner so they could see their son and catch up on any gossip.

Mandy loved seeing Nanny and Granfy, they were always so pleased to see her; and with Daddy being home as well these nights were always so special.

Ruby and Derek Croft were the envy of many of their friends and family, they weren't particularly well off, but they were happy. The council house they lived in was well decorated and to top it all they had the most beautiful baby daughter in the world.

The Crofts often held dinner parties – Ruby loved entertaining. These parties were also a good excuse for her to show off her prized garden! She revelled in the praise she received for all the hard work she had put into it. Why not? She deserved it.

Life for the Croft family was happy, and as usual Ruby came home with Mandy after her morning at playschool, before preparing to make lunch.

"What would you like in your sandwich, sweetheart?"

"Chocolate spread Mummy!" came the reply from upstairs. Mandy had rushed in and headed straight for her bedroom where Katy, her favourite doll was waiting on her bed.

"I don't know why I ask you, it's the same answer every day" laughed Ruby as she opened the cupboard door. At that moment the phone rang. She rushed into the lounge and picked up the receiver.

"Could I please speak to Mrs Ruby Croft," said an official sounding voice.

"Speaking!" replied Ruby.

"Mrs Croft, this is Jack Wilson, I have some bad news for you."

"Go on, I'm listening," said Ruby quietly, knowing that Jack Wilson only rang if there was a serious problem. A wave of dread overcame her.

"There's been an accident. Derek was repairing some pipes when the scaffolding he was on gave way. He became trapped underneath."

"Is…is he okay? I'll make arrangements and fly out straight away. Which hospital is he at?"

"Mrs Croft I'm afraid Derek died at the scene."

"Oh my God, no. He can't be dead. He's coming home next week; we're going Christmas shopping. You've got the wrong man, my Derek's not dead!"

"If there's anything I can do, Mrs Croft. I know this is a great shock to you and you have the sympathy of everyone here on the rig."

"I just can't believe it! What will we do without him? What do I say to Mandy?" Oh no, Mandy. At that moment Ruby remembered her daughter playing happily upstairs. How do you tell a four-year-old girl that her beloved father is gone?

"I'm sorry but I've got to see to my daughter, can you phone back later? I need to get this into my head before I can think about what to do next."

"Of course, Mrs Croft. I'll ring back tomorrow; but in the meantime if there's anything you need please don't hesitate to phone me here at the rig. Do you have the number?"

"Yes, Derek always leaves, sorry – left, the number by the phone in case of emergencies. Thanks for phoning." Ruby replaced the handset and sat down on the nearby sofa. She put her hands over her face and then lent forward resting her head on her knees. She was in complete disbelief of the conversation she had just had. It was like one of those tragic films they show on daytime television Ruby stayed with her head buried in her hands for about five minutes until she was startled by a little voice from upstairs.

"Is my lunch ready Mummy?" called Mandy to her mum, blissfully unaware that she had just lost one of the two most important people in her life.

"Sorry sweetheart, come down and I'll do it now." Ruby returned to the kitchen. As she prepared Mandy's sandwich she noticed that her hands were shaking uncontrollably. The shock of what she had just heard was setting in.

As she placed the sandwich on the table Mandy skipped into the kitchen singing 'Baa baa black sheep' which she had learned at school that morning. Ruby turned in silence to fetch a drink for her daughter. She poured some squash into a glass and went to the tap to dilute it. She turned the tap too much and the water gushed into the glass with such a force that it splashed straight out again all over her hands and the sink.

"Oh, this stupid bloody tap!" shouted Ruby as she placed the glass down on the side and dropped to her knees in tears.

"What is it Mummy?" Mandy walked over to her mum and put her little arms around her. Ruby turned and hugged her tightly. After a couple of minutes she faced her daughter, held both her hands and took a deep breath. This was not going to be easy.

"My darling daughter, I have some very bad news for you. Daddy had an accident at work."

"Is he in hospital? Did he need a plaster? He can have one of my dolly plasters, they won't mind!"

"Listen to me Mandy, Daddy was hurt badly so he went to hospital. He fell asleep at hospital and they couldn't wake him up. He's gone to Heaven." Ruby could hear her voice trembling as she spoke.

Mandy looked up at her mother. "Daddy can't be in Heaven, only old people go there and Daddy's not old!

"Old people and special people," replied Ruby. "And your Daddy is the most special person in the world. We have to be strong now and remember how lucky we were to have him."

"Can I play outside Mummy, I don't want my lunch now?" said Mandy, quietly.

"Of course you can sweetie." Ruby reached for Mandy's coat, which was hanging on the back door handle and helped her to put it on. "You know where I am if you need me. I love you Mandy."

"Love you too, Mummy; and I love Daddy in Heaven too!" replied Mandy as she walked slowly out of the back door. Ruby struggled to hold back the tears as she watched her daughter head for her swing. She switched on the kettle to make a cup of tea. Wasn't that supposed to help at times like these? As she did so the doorbell rang.

"We came straight over when we heard. Jack Wilson at the rig phoned us," said Joyce as she put her arms around her daughter-in-law. How's Mandy? Have you told her?

"Yes, just," answered Ruby, holding the door for Joyce and Viv to enter. "I don't know if she really understands though; she's outside on her swing. I thought it best to let her deal with it in her own way. If she needs me she knows I'm here for her. I've just put the kettle on."

"Just you sit down, I'll make the tea. You two ladies go and sit in the lounge and I'll bring it in. At least I'll be doing something useful," Viv interrupted, as he took three mugs from a cupboard. Ruby and Joyce headed for the lounge and sat on the sofa.

"What are we going to do without him, Joyce? I can't get my head round this. I keep expecting the phone to ring and hear his voice on the other end telling me it was all a big mistake, they've got the wrong person."

"We have to be strong, it's not going to be easy but we have to for Mandy's sake," replied Joyce. Ruby only had Joyce and Viv for support. She had been an only child and had lost her parents at the age of twelve in a car crash. She was put into foster care but had rebelled as a teenager and once old enough left home and lived in bedsits until she met Derek at the age of seventeen. They had been together ever since.

The next few days were a blur. Arrangements were made to bring Derek's body back home to Bournemouth and the funeral was organised. Derek was a popular figure in the local area, and this was reflected by the amount of sympathy cards and spoken condolences that Ruby received.

Mandy stayed home from playschool until after the funeral. She had been very quiet since that awful day she found out she would not see Daddy again and Ruby was rather worried about her. Ruby herself was coping remarkably well. With the support of Viv and Joyce she managed to get through. She even managed to lay on a delicious spread for after the funeral service.

"If this is the last thing I'm going to do for my Derek then I'm going to do him proud!" Ruby told everyone. And she did. There must have been forty – fifty people in the chapel that morning; friends from Derek's past, distant relatives, even work colleagues from the rig. Everybody came back to the house afterwards.

Although it was a sad occasion, there was a good atmosphere that afternoon. It was what Derek would have wanted. He was never one for being miserable and would be the first one to make a party out of any occasion, even his own funeral!

Mandy didn't really understand why everyone was so happy: she wouldn't see Daddy again so why should she be happy about it? By early evening the wake was still in full swing but Mandy was getting tired.

"Can I go to bed Mummy?"

"Of course, sweetie. It's been a long day and you must be exhausted." Ruby picked her daughter up and carried her up the stairs.

"What happens when everyone goes home, Mummy?" asked Mandy.

"It's just you and me then, sweetie! We'll show everybody that we can manage on our own. We're going to have the best of everything even if Daddy's not here to share it with us, just you wait and see."

Ruby kissed her young daughter on the cheek and quietly made her way out of the bedroom. In the back of her mind Ruby began to wonder how on earth she was going to cope and what the future now had in store for the two of them.

Chapter 2

The next couple of weeks were difficult for Ruby; Christmas was creeping nearer and she just couldn't bring herself round to think about it. She and Derek always did the Christmas shopping together. Mandy would go to Nanny and Granfy's for the day and they would drive up to Southampton. Here they could usually get everything in one go and in plenty of time before the Christmas rush. This year though, Ruby couldn't face it. She had become very depressed and hadn't been out of the house since the funeral, not even to take Mandy to school.

Joyce visited a couple of times but couldn't get through to Ruby.

"Why don't you let Mandy come and stay with us for a while?" she suggested.

"I could take her to playschool for you and get her back into some kind of routine, she must be missing her friends."

Ruby took offence at this suggestion.

"Do you think I can't cope?" she snapped.

"I'm only trying to help, Ruby."

"We don't need your help or anyone else's for that matter! Why don't you all just leave us alone?"

"Okay Ruby, if that's what you want. You may have just lost your husband but please remember he was my son and I feel as upset as you do. You know where we are if you need us." With that Joyce left.

Ruby sat at the kitchen table and burst into tears. She didn't mean to snap at Joyce but lately she just couldn't control her temper. Why did Derek have to die? It just wasn't fair. They had such a good life with so much to look forward to. How could she and Mandy ever be happy now?

After an hour or so she telephoned Joyce.

"I'm so sorry for shouting at you, it was totally un-called for."

"Don't worry my dear, it's completely understandable," replied Joyce. "I've been exactly the same, one minute okay and the next in tears. It's going to take time."

"I've thought about your suggestion though, Joyce," said Ruby. "I think it may be a good idea if Mandy comes to stay with you for a while. It's not fair on her to be shut in the house with me like this. With you and Viv she'll have company. It will also give me a chance to sort through Derek's things without upsetting her."

"That's no problem, Ruby. Why don't we pick her up tomorrow? It will give you a chance to get her things together and spend the evening with each other."

Ruby agreed and after putting the phone down went upstairs to tell Mandy what was happening. Mandy was pleased to be going to Nanny and Granfy's but was a little concerned about leaving her mum on her own.

"Will you be alright, Mummy? Can't you come to Nanny's with me?"

"I'll be fine, sweetie. I've got a few things to do here. Don't worry about me, just make sure

Nanny and Granfy are okay I promise I'll phone every night before you go to bed."

Mandy seemed reassured and so they spent the afternoon packing her clothes and favourite toys. After tea they sat together on the sofa looking through old photos and remembering the good times spent as a family. Being only four years old Mandy didn't remember most of it, but she sat quietly while her mum talked about what they did on these wonderful days. Eventually Mandy fell asleep in her mother's arms and Ruby carried her up to bed. As she tucked her daughter in, the tears welled up in Ruby's eyes. She was going to miss Mandy.

After coming back downstairs Ruby packed away the photo albums, walked over to the mini-bar, which they used when they had their dinner parties and poured herself a glass of vodka. It was unusual for Ruby to drink. Even at their parties she would only have one glass of wine and then lemonade or orange juice. She glanced at the clock on the wall. It was only 8.20, the evenings were so long now. Outside it was a typical November night, cold, wet and windy.

Ruby switched on the television and sat down on the sofa. Nicholas Parsons was showing another showcase of prizes on 'Sale of the Century.' She sat watching the screen although not really taking in what was going on. She took a large sip from her glass. The vodka almost burned as she drank. Almost straightaway Ruby put the glass to her lips again. This time she finished off the contents of the glass in one go. As she sat back she felt the effects of the alcohol reach her head.

She sat back in the chair. It was the first time since Derek's death that she had felt calm. It felt good. At this moment nothing else mattered. She closed her eyes and relaxed. Within minutes Ruby fell into a deep sleep, only to be woken up just after midnight by the high-pitched noise on the television, signalling the end of that day's transmission. She stood up, switched off the television and lounge light and took herself up to bed.

Mandy woke up early the next morning, eager to see Nanny and Granfy. She ran into her mum's bedroom.

"Hello Mummy, I'm going to Nanny's today!" she announced.

Ruby opened her eyes slowly.

"Good morning sweetie," she replied to her daughter. As she sat up she felt a throbbing in her head. It must have been that vodka last night, she thought to herself.

"Why don't you go downstairs sweetie? I'll be down in a minute."

"Okay Mummy," Mandy replied as she headed for the stairs.

Ruby sat on the edge of the bed.

"I'd better take some aspirin if this headache's going to go," she thought to herself. "Still, I've only got myself to blame."

Ruby got herself dressed and went down to the kitchen where Mandy was waiting. She put some bread into the toaster and while waiting for it to brown took some aspirin.

"What's the matter, Mummy?" asked Mandy.

"It's just a bit of a headache, nothing to worry about. Are you all set for today then?"

"Yes, Mummy. I've just got to pack Katy and my other dollies and then I'm ready."

At 10 o'clock Joyce arrived and Mandy eagerly helped to put her bags in the car. Although she was happy to be going to Nanny and Granfy's she was going to miss Mummy and was worried about leaving her on her own.

"Come on then, darling," said Joyce. "We'd better go now as we've got some shopping to do on the way."

Mandy held her mum's hand as they walked up to the car. Ruby hugged her and told her to be good. As they drove off she walked backed into the house, feeling a sudden emptiness inside. She went into the lounge and headed for the mini-bar where she poured herself a glass of vodka.

She took first one sip and then another. Then she finished the glass.

"Come on, pull yourself together," Ruby said to herself as she sat on the sofa. " This is no way to go on."

She made her way into the kitchen and put the glass into the sink.

"Right then," Ruby announced to herself, "this house needs sorting."

She spent the rest of the day tidying up, bagging up Derek's clothes to take to the charity shop, polishing every room in the house, stripping

Mandy's bed and putting what toys she had left behind away.

By late afternoon Ruby realised that she was hungry. There wasn't much in the house so she decided to walk up to the corner shop to find something to eat. It was the first time that she had gone out of the house since Derek died. Joyce had been bringing groceries up to now. It was also the first time she had gone out with no make-up on. She was always so immaculately turned out and wouldn't dream of leaving the house without at least some mascara on!

"Hello Mrs Croft," said Nigel the shop owner. "I'm so sorry to hear about Derek. How are you and Mandy coping?"

"I think we're doing okay thanks, Nigel," replied Ruby. "Mandy's gone to stay with her Grandparents for a while so that I can get things straight at home."

"If you need anything you know where I am, I know it's not easy." Nigel had lost his wife to cancer three years before and so had some idea what she was going through.

"Thanks Nigel, I appreciate it," replied Ruby as she picked up a loaf of bread, some eggs and a pint of milk. She walked over to the counter and while Nigel totalled up on the till she looked behind him at the display of alcohol on the shelf.

"Can I have a small bottle of vodka as well, please?"

"Certainly," replied Nigel as he placed a bottle in the carrier with the other items. Ruby paid for her things, said goodbye and walked back home.

By now it was about 6 p.m. Ruby made herself some scrambled egg on toast and sat at the kitchen table. The house felt so quiet and empty without Mandy. She finished her meal, went into the lounge and picked up the phone.

"Is that you, Mummy?" asked the little voice at the other end of the line.

"Yes, sweetie, are you okay?

"Yes, Mummy. We went shopping and bought some cakes and sweets. Tomorrow Nanny's taking me to the park if it's not too cold! And next week I'm going to help Nanny put the Christmas decorations up!"

"Sounds like you're going to be busy then, sweetie!" exclaimed Ruby, "Try not to wear Nanny out too much!"

"I won't, Mummy. I'm going to have a bath and go to bed now. Will you phone me tomorrow?"

"Yes, of course I will," replied Ruby. "Off you go for your bath then and I'll speak to you tomorrow. Goodnight sweetie."

"Goodnight, Mummy," came the reply.

Ruby replaced the handset. She now felt so lonely. Outside it was dark and beginning to rain. She walked over to the large bay window and drew the curtains. She then switched on the television but didn't even look to see what program was on.

Before she sat down, Ruby went over to the mini-bar on top of which she had placed the new vodka bottle. She poured herself a large measure and sat down. Within ten minutes she had finished the glass and poured herself another. As on the previous evening, Ruby closed her eyes and fell asleep. When she was woken again by the transmission signal she got up, switched off the television and laid back down on the sofa. Here she stayed until the next morning, when she woke up with a pounding headache.

Ruby spent most of the following day lying on the sofa, not even getting up to read the post or open the curtains. She did get up around 6 p.m. to make herself some toast and to phone Mandy, but after she had spoken to her daughter found herself once again sitting in the lounge with a glass of vodka in her hand. A pattern was beginning to emerge, and not a very happy one.

This routine continued for the next couple of weeks, with Ruby only getting up to go to the shop for another bottle, or to telephone her daughter.

Meanwhile, at Joyce's house Mandy was as happy as ever. They went to the park, as promised. They went Christmas shopping where Joyce gave Mandy some money to buy her mum a present. She chose a beautiful gold pendant with 'Best Mummy' etched on a heart.

It was now only a week to Christmas and Mandy helped her nanny to put up the tree and decorations.

"Can Mummy come here for Christmas?" Mandy asked as they put the finishing touches to the tree.

"Of course, darling. When she phones tonight we'll ask her."

Christmas Day arrived. Mandy stayed with her Granfy while Joyce went to collect Ruby. When she arrived Ruby was still in her dressing gown. She hadn't even bothered to have a wash or to brush her hair.

"I'm sorry, Ruby. Am I too early?"

"No, Joyce, I had a bit of a bad night last night. I'll be okay in a while. Come in, I'll get myself ready."

Joyce couldn't believe what she saw when Ruby let her in the door. As she walked into the hallway and through to the kitchen she saw the pile of mugs, plates and cutlery that had been there for days. There was an awful smell coming from the waste bin, which was overflowing. There were saucepans on the side with dried-in baked beans, and a half-used loaf of bread, which had gone mouldy.

"I'm sorry about the mess, Joyce," Ruby said before Joyce had the chance to comprehend what she was looking at. "I've been feeling a bit under the weather lately and have got a bit behind with the housework."

"You can say that again, Ruby."

Joyce turned to her daughter-in-law.

"Go and get yourself dressed, I'll clear up down here," she ordered as she began emptying the dirty crockery from the sink.

"Don't worry about the washing up, I can do that tonight when I come home," Ruby protested.

"It won't take me five minutes," replied Joyce, "and anyway, you won't want to do it when you come home."

"Okay" answered Ruby as she headed for the stairs. She didn't have the energy to argue.

Joyce washed the dishes that were in the kitchen and then went into the lounge to see if there was anything else to wash. She opened the curtains, which were still closed and turned around.

"Oh my God!" Joyce whispered to herself as she saw the state of the lounge. There must have been at least twelve empty vodka bottles on the mini-bar. There were another two on the floor in front of the sofa. There were empty glasses on the coffee table, two plates with the dried up remains of sandwiches on them and empty biscuit packets. The was also a blanket thrown on the sofa which Ruby had used to keep warm at night when she couldn't be bothered to take herself up to bed.

Joyce took the glasses and plates into the kitchen and returned with a large bin liner into which she put the empty bottles, leftovers and wrappers. She took the bag outside the back door to where the dustbin was. When she returned Ruby was just coming down the stairs.

"What has got into you, Ruby?" asked Joyce sternly. "You're supposed to be sorting things out, not getting yourself drunk every night! I'm just glad poor little Mandy isn't here to see you like this."

"Nothing's got into me," replied Ruby defensively. "I've had a few drinks. What's wrong with that?"

"I'm not getting into an argument with you today, Ruby. It's Christmas and you've a little girl waiting for you so she can open her presents."

Joyce finished washing the glasses and wiped the sides down while Ruby picked up a tea towel and dried up what was left. No one said a word until they were finished.

"Are you ready then?" asked Joyce as the last of the glasses were taken back to the bar in the lounge.

"Yes, let's go."

Ruby and Joyce drove in silence the twenty-minute journey back to Joyce's house. When they arrived Ruby was greeted by shouts of "Mummy, Mummy" by her daughter.

"Merry Christmas sweetie," said Ruby as she knelt down to give her young daughter a big hug.

"Mummy, Mummy, you've got to see the pile of presents. There's loads and loads! Nanny's making a big Christmas dinner for us and she's made a big Christmas cake." Mandy took her mother's hand and led her down the garden path to the front door. "We can open our presents now you're here!"

"Come on then, sweetie, what are we waiting for?" Ruby replied as they went indoors followed by Joyce. Ruby was struggling to keep up with her daughter's enthusiasm; she had an enormous hangover but hadn't dared to tell Joyce. She could only imagine the grief that would have caused!

"You two go into the lounge and I'll make a cup of tea," said Joyce, "or would you rather have a strong coffee Ruby?"

Ruby sensed the sarcasm in Joyce's voice.

"No, tea will be fine, thank you," she replied, glaring at Joyce.

Ruby followed Mandy into the lounge where Viv greeted them.

"Hello Ruby, how are you?" asked Viv. Ruby had always got on well with Viv. He was the sought of person everyone liked. He didn't have a bad word to say about anyone. Viv was so much like his son Derek, which was probably why Ruby liked him so much.

"I'm fine, thanks Viv," answered Ruby.

"You do look rather tired, are you sleeping okay?

"Not really, but I think once Christmas is over and everything is back to normal I'll be fine."

At that moment Joyce walked in with the tea on a tray.

"Let's just hope it does get back to normal, eh, Ruby?" she said as she placed the tray on the coffee table. Ruby knew exactly what Joyce meant but chose to ignore the remark.

"Come on then Mandy, let's get these presents open." Ruby said to her daughter. Ruby sat on the sofa next to Viv while Mandy placed herself on the floor in front of them. Joyce sat on the single chair, which was next to the Christmas tree, from where she could reach the presents piled around it. Mandy could hardly contain her excitement as she opened her presents. She received a new doll to add to her collection, colouring books and crayons, new pyjamas, numerous selection boxes and hair accessories. Joyce had also bought Ruby a box of chocolates and a jewellery box.

Ruby felt guilty because she hadn't even written a card for Viv and Joyce.

"Don't worry my dear," said Viv when Ruby apologised, "you've been through enough without having to worry about getting us anything. As long as little Mandy's happy that's all that matters. Isn't that right Joyce?"

"Yes dear. Don't worry; *I've* made sure Mandy's okay this year." Joyce gave Ruby a disapproving glance as she reached another present for Mandy. Viv was beginning to sense an atmosphere between his wife and daughter in law.

"Come on, it's Christmas, a time of good will, remember?" he said. "Mandy, where's that special present you bought for Mummy?

"It's upstairs, I'll just go and get it," replied Mandy as she ran out of the room and up the stairs.

Viv took his chance while Mandy was out of the room.

"I don't know what's going on between you two but I don't like it," he said quietly, "It's hard for all of us but we have to make the best of it, and bitching at each other won't help."

"Nor will drinking herself silly every night!" snapped Joyce looking toward Ruby.

"So I've had a few drinks. What else is there to do when I'm stuck in that house on my own? It's not like I'm an alcoholic!"

"Looking at the state of that lounge this morning I'm not so sure," replied Joyce. She turned to Viv.

"You should have seen it, empty vodka bottles all over the place. She hadn't even bothered to hide the evidence…" Joyce was about to say something else when they heard Mandy's footsteps coming down the stairs.

"Here it is Mummy, "said Mandy as she placed a small package in Ruby's hand. Ruby opened the wrapper, which revealed a small plastic gift box. She opened the box and looked to find the gold heart shaped pendant inside. As she read the inscription 'Best Mummy' she began to cry.

"Oh Mandy sweetie, it's beautiful."

"I chose it all by myself, Mummy. Do you like it?"

"I love it, and I love you. Come here and give me a hug."

As Mandy hugged her mother Joyce arose from her chair.

"Mummy's got a present for you too, Mandy. You'll have to come outside, though because it's too big to bring into the house."

Mandy grabbed Ruby's hand and they went out to the back garden followed by Viv and Joyce. As she stepped out of the door Mandy couldn't believe her eyes! Her first proper bike! It was bright pink with stabilisers. The handlebars had brightly coloured tassels hanging from them, and there was a basket on the front. Tied around the bike was a large pink ribbon, attached to which was a small card. Mandy took the card and handed it to Ruby.

"What does this say, Mummy?" she asked eagerly. Ruby took the card and read it out loud.

"To Mandy, Happy Christmas with all my love, Mummy."

"Thank you Mummy, can I ride it now?" Mandy asked excitedly.

"Of course you can sweetie," Ruby answered as her daughter climbed on it and pedalled unsteadily to the end of the garden. She turned to Joyce.

"Thanks Joyce, it's lovely. I don't think I could have chosen better if I'd gone out to get it myself."

Viv stayed outside with Mandy while the two women headed back inside.

"I'll put the kettle on, would you like another tea, Ruby?" asked Joyce.

"I wouldn't mind, thank you."

There was an awkward silence before Ruby spoke.

"Look Joyce, I know how it seems but I was only drinking because I was lonely. With Mandy here with you the house is so quiet and I can't seem to get myself motivated. I'm really missing her."

Joyce sympathised with Ruby. The two women had a good heart to heart talk about Derek and how they were coping without him. They also talked about Ruby and her drinking. Ruby managed to convince Joyce that it was only through boredom and that once Mandy was home it would stop. It was agreed that Mandy would stay another couple of days and then return home to her mother.

"We had better tell Mandy the good news," said Joyce as both women rose from their seats. They went into the back garden where Viv was sat on the seat watching his Granddaughter. Mandy was cycling round and round the large lawn.

"Look at me, Mummy, I can ride a bike like big children!" shouted Mandy to her mother.

"That's wonderful, sweetie," replied Ruby. "Why don't you ride over this way, I've got some good news for you."

"What is it Mummy?" Mandy asked as she steered the bike towards Ruby. As she arrived at where Ruby was stood Mandy scraped her shoes along the ground and came to a stop.

"I think you need some practise with those brakes," laughed Ruby as she jumped out of the way. "Listen Mandy, how would you like to come back home with me? I've sorted the house out now. The only thing missing is you!"

"Yes, yes. I want to see my teddies and my other dollies again! When am I coming home, Mummy?"

"How about if you stay with Nanny and Granfy tonight and spend tomorrow with them as its Boxing Day. I can go to the shops the day after and make sure there's food in the house for us, and perhaps Nanny can drop you home in the afternoon."

It was all agreed and the rest of Christmas Day was spent playing board games and dollies. By late afternoon Joyce had prepared the most enormous Christmas dinner you had ever seen, with all the trimmings; a huge turkey, stuffing, sausages wrapped in bacon, roast parsnips and more roast potatoes than would fit on their plates! This was topped only by Joyce's homemade Christmas pudding and Brandy Custard. Mandy wasn't keen on Christmas pudding so Joyce had made her an individual portion of strawberry ice cream with wafers, topped with hundreds and thousands.

"This is the best Christmas ever," announced Mandy as the ice cream was placed in front of her. "I wish Daddy was here though."

"We all do, sweetie," replied Ruby. "But I'm sure Daddy's up there in Heaven having a bigger Christmas dinner than us. You know how much he enjoyed roast turkey!"

The room was quiet as dessert was eaten and their thoughts went to Derek. Christmas would never be the same without him. The grief was still very much present after such a short time.

When everyone had finished Joyce and Ruby washed the dishes while Mandy kept Viv busy colouring with her new crayons. When the washing up was finished they all settled down in front of the television to watch 'The Wizard of Oz'. Mandy had a glass of lemonade while the three adults had a glass of wine each. The taste of alcohol was a very welcome one to Ruby. Unknown to Joyce or Viv she had started drinking in the daytime as well. By the time the film finished Mandy was drifting off to sleep, so she said goodnight to Mummy and Granfy, and Joyce took her up to bed.

"I won't see you in the morning, sweetie," said Ruby as she gave her daughter a goodnight hug. "But I'll phone you tomorrow night to make sure you're ready to come home the next day.

Within a couple of minutes of Mandy's head touching the pillow she had drifted off into a lovely deep sleep. Ruby decided now was a good time to say her goodbyes. Viv offered her a lift but she declined and phoned for a taxi.

"It's Christmas and you should be relaxing, Viv, not running me about," she said as she put the phone down. The cab will be here in ten minutes."

Ruby turned to Joyce.

"Thanks for everything Joyce," she said as she put on her coat. "I don't think I could have got through today without you both."

"Will you be alright tonight and tomorrow?" Joyce asked.

"Yes, thanks. I've got something to look forward to now, Mandy coming back home."

Chapter 3

Ruby paid the taxi driver and walked down the pathway to her front door. The house was in complete darkness and as she switched on the hall light she realised she was alone again. She walked into the lounge and closed the curtains. She turned towards the mini-bar and then stopped.

"Don't you dare," Ruby said to herself. "Mandy's coming home, pull yourself together." She walked out of the lounge, into the kitchen and filled the kettle with water. "A coffee will do far more good than alcohol."

Ruby sat at the kitchen table and drank her coffee. She thought about how the day had gone and was pleased that Mandy had enjoyed herself so much. She was so looking forward to having her back home again and vowed to herself not to drink anymore for the sake of her daughter. When her cup was empty Ruby rinsed it out and after switching the lights off went upstairs to her bedroom. She went to the window to draw the curtains and as she looked out she could see the houses along the street, all lit up with Christmas lights. Where some still had their curtains open she could see people dancing, eating and drinking.

"Things are going to be different from now on," Ruby promised herself as she closed the curtains and got into bed. She turned off the bedside light and lay for a long while thinking about Mandy and the future before falling asleep.

Mandy returned the day after Boxing Day as promised. She was glad to be home again. Ruby had made Spaghetti Bolognese, Mandy's favourite meal. When Derek was alive he and Mandy would have contests to see who could suck up the longest piece of spaghetti. Invariably they would both end up with Bolognese sauce all over their clothes, much to Ruby's disgust! After dinner Ruby helped Mandy to put away all her new Christmas presents. Mandy was very particular about where her toys were put. She had a special place for everything. When the room was sorted out Ruby ran a bath for her daughter. They chatted while Mandy washed herself and her mum washed her hair.

"How would you like to go back to playschool after the New Year, sweetie?" asked Ruby as she wrapped a large bath towel around Mandy and rubbed her dry.

"Yes, Mummy. I can tell everyone what I got for Christmas!"

"I expect your friends have missed you," said Ruby as she reached for the clean pair if pyjamas she had put out ready. When Mandy was dressed Ruby tucked her into bed and gave her a goodnight kiss.

"It's wonderful to have you home again. It's been so quiet here without you," she said as she turned off the light.

"Goodnight, Mummy."

The rest of the Christmas holiday went by fairly quickly. Ruby managed to refrain from drinking and keep her head together, even in the evenings once Mandy had gone to bed. Mandy went back to playschool three mornings a week and settled back into a routine. Joyce popped in or telephoned every now and then just to make sure everything was o.k, which it was until February 14th – Valentine's Day and what should have been Derek and Ruby's wedding anniversary.

The day started well; Mandy went to playschool as usual while Ruby decided to go into Bournemouth to do some shopping to keep her mind occupied. As she looked in the various shop windows though, all she could see were reminders of what day it was. Every window seemed to be adorned with hearts and flowers, inviting shoppers to come in and see their 'Special Valentine Offers'. The jewellers shop were promoting sets of engagement and wedding rings for the countless couples who would set a date tonight; and the card shops were full of heart-shaped balloons, and teddies holding heart-shaped cushions with 'Be My Valentine' or 'To The One I Love' written on them. The final straw for Ruby came when she walked past the old gypsy flower seller who had a stall right in the centre of Bournemouth Square.

"Come on, all you young men, get your flowers here!" the old man was shouting as she walked past.

"How about you, Madam, I bet your man's bought you flowers hasn't he?"
Ruby just looked at the old man and then ran back to the car park. She unlocked the door of her car, and as she sat in the seat the tears came flooding out. Ruby bowed her head and hands to the steering wheel and sobbed uncontrollably for a good ten to fifteen minutes. When she did finally stop she looked at her watch. 11.30. It was time to collect

Mandy from school. She took a piece of tissue from her handbag and wiped her eyes. Looking in the rear view mirror Ruby could see that her mascara had run down her cheeks. She wiped it off as best she could with the tissue and hoped that none of the other mothers at school would notice.

She arrived at the playschool about five minutes late, which meant that most of the mothers would have already gone. The teacher noticed her red eyes and asked if she was all right.

"Yes I'm fine, thanks," replied Ruby. "I've just had one of those mornings but I'm okay now." She tried to sound as cheerful as she could; the last thing she needed was the school thinking she couldn't cope. Mandy came out with a large model she had made with an egg box, cereal packet and two yoghurt cartons glued together.

"Look Mummy, I've made a car!"

"That's wonderful, sweetie." said Ruby as she carefully took the model from Mandy. "We'll have to find a safe place for this, won't we?" They said goodbye to the teacher and made their way back to the car. When they arrived home Mandy asked for her usual chocolate spread sandwich. They sat and ate lunch together and then Mandy played outside on her new bike. She never seemed to notice the cold: it couldn't have been much above freezing. Ruby washed and cleared away the lunch plates and went into the lounge. She switched on the television and sat on the sofa. 'House Party' had just started, and one of the presenters was being shown how to make a winter soup. Ruby wasn't really interested in the television but couldn't get herself motivated to do anything else. Her eyes wandered over to the mini-bar and for the first time since Mandy had come back home she got up and poured herself a vodka.

"After the morning I've had I deserve it," said Ruby to herself as she took the first sip, "and anyway what harm will one little drink do?" Unfortunately though, one little drink became two little drinks, then three; and before she knew it, Ruby had finished off the bottle and was completely drunk by the time Mandy had come in from outside an hour or so later.

"Is it tea time yet, Mummy?" asked Mandy. By this time Ruby was lying on the sofa, barely coherent. She opened her eyes and looked at her young daughter, slurring as she spoke.

"In a minute, sweetie. Go and play in your room." Mandy wasn't sure what to make of her mother. She had never seen her like this.

"Are you alright, Mummy?" she asked worriedly.

"I'm fine, go and play."

Mandy did as she was told and went upstairs to play with her dolls. It was about 5p.m. when Ruby struggled to sit up, her head spinning if she moved too fast. Once upright she sat for a while and then attempted to stand. Her legs were like jelly and she fell back down on the sofa. On the second attempt Ruby managed to stay up and staggered to the kitchen. She took some bread from the bread bin and put it into the toaster. She then took a tin of baked beans out of the cupboard and found the tin opener.

"Damn this bloody opener," Ruby cursed as she struggled to turn the handle and open the tin. By the time she had done it the toast had already popped out if the toaster. She grabbed a saucepan from the rack in the corner of the kitchen and poured the beans into it, spilling about a third of the contents over the worktop. Without bothering to clean up the mess she took the pan over to the cooker where she attempted to light the gas burner. There was always a box of matches on the worktop next to the cooker. Ruby picked up the box and as she pushed the insert the matches fell all over the floor.

She swore under her breath as she knelt down to pick them up. She managed to pick most of the matches up but tried to get up too quickly and fell on the floor. Slowly Ruby managed to get herself up using the cupboards and worktop for support. The next problem was lighting a match. The first two snapped in half where Ruby pressed too hard on the box. She managed to light the third but it went out again before she could get it to the burner. Finally with the fourth match Ruby lit the burner and placed the saucepan over the flame. While the beans were heating up she took a plate from the cupboard and a knife and fork from the drawer. The toast, which by now was cold was put on the plate before Ruby went back to pick up the saucepan of beans. She clumsily poured the beans over the toast and called to Mandy as she put the plate on the table.

"Mummy you've left the cooker on," Mandy pointed out as she sat at the table. Ruby said nothing as she turned off the gas and walked straight past her daughter and out of the kitchen without even acknowledging that she was there. Mandy was puzzled by the way her mum was acting. Had she done something wrong? She couldn't think of anything. Normally Ruby would sit at the table with her daughter and they would talk about what they had done that day, but today for some reason Mummy wasn't very happy. Mandy ate her meal in silence and then went into the lounge to see her mum, who by now was lying asleep on the sofa. She nudged her gently but couldn't wake her, so she nudged her a bit harder. This still made no difference so Mandy went upstairs to play with her dolls. She played for a couple of hours until she became tired.

"It must be bed time," she thought to herself although she couldn't tell the time yet, so she put her nightdress on and went downstairs to say goodnight to her mum. Ruby was still fast asleep on the sofa, and as hard as she tried, Mandy could not wake her up. She took herself up to bed.

"Mummy will be up soon," she thought to herself as she pulled the covers over, but before Ruby did wake up Mandy fell into a deep sleep.

Ruby did eventually wake up about 9p.m. She sat up but was disorientated for a while before looking at the clock on the mantelpiece. She suddenly thought about her daughter.

"Mandy!" She called out but received no reply. Slowly Ruby stood up and went upstairs, holding the banister tightly so as not to fall. She quietly put her head round Mandy's bedroom door and saw the top of her tiny head peeping out from under the blanket. She crept over to the bed and leaned over to kiss her daughter on the head.

"I'm so sorry, sweetie," Ruby whispered. "It won't happen again." She went back downstairs, washed the few dishes that were there and made herself a strong coffee. She went back into the lounge where the television announcer was introducing the film, which was about to start. What other film could they show on Valentine's Day apart from 'Love Story?'

"I'm not watching this!" announced Ruby to herself as she switched off the television, turned off the lounge light and went up to bed.

Ruby was awake before Mandy the next morning. She had already prepared breakfast by the time she had come downstairs.

"Good morning, sweetie," said Ruby.

"I didn't say goodnight to you, last night, Mummy! You were asleep and I couldn't wake you up."

"Yes I know, and I'm sorry. I did come up and give you a kiss though. I had a bad day yesterday. It won't happen again, I promise." Ruby sat with Mandy while she ate her breakfast.

"As you've not got playschool today would you like to help me with the food shopping?" Ruby asked her daughter.

"Can we buy some sweeties?" asked Mandy excitedly.

"Of course we can. Come on then, let's get going before it gets too busy." They finished breakfast and headed for the local supermarket.

Mandy loved shopping. Although she was four, she was still small enough to sit in the trolley. She would point at all the colourful packages and tins, choosing her favourite cereals and biscuits. When they reached the confectionery aisle Mandy was spoilt for choice.

"What would you like then sweetie?" asked Ruby.

"Can I have these? No, wait a minute, those." Mandy had spotted the brightly coloured packet of 'Spangles'.

"Are you sure?" laughed Ruby as she picked up the packet, "Or are you going to change your mind again?" Mandy had made her decision and so they carried on with the shopping.

"Almost finished now," said Ruby as they walked through the wines and spirit section. Without even thinking about it she picked up two large bottles of vodka and placed them in the trolley. They carried on to the fruit and vegetable section and picked up the last of the shopping and then headed for the checkout. Ruby paid for the groceries and they headed back home. Once home, Mandy played for an hour or so until lunchtime while her mum put away the shopping and made herself some coffee.

After lunch Ruby took Mandy to visit Viv and Joyce. They were pleased to see their Granddaughter, they didn't see as much of her now as they did before.

"It's good to see you Ruby," said Joyce as she made a cup of tea, "how are you managing?"

"Fine thanks, Joyce," replied Ruby.

"You're not drinking, I hope."

"I haven't touched a drop since Mandy's been home." Ruby's eyes looked away from Joyce as she spoke. She didn't dare say anything about the day before, and anyway it was a 'one-off' she told herself. Joyce invited Ruby and Mandy to stay for dinner, which they did. It was about 8p.m. by the time they returned home.

"Come on then, its bedtime," said Ruby as they took off their coats, "you've got school in the morning." It wasn't long before Mandy was tucked up in bed and fast asleep, and not much longer after that before Ruby was once again sat on the sofa with a glass of vodka in her hand. Within an hour she was too drunk to take herself up to bed and so spent yet another night on the sofa with a blanket over her.

It was about 7.30 the next morning when Mandy came down the stairs. At the bottom of the stairs she noticed the lounge door was open so she went in.

"Mummy, it's time to get up now," said Mandy as she nudged her mum.

"Not now, go away," replied Ruby as she buried her head under the blanket.

"I've got school today, Mummy. Can you get my breakfast?"

Ruby raised her head and looked angrily at Mandy.

"For Christ's sake, didn't you hear me? I said go away. You're not going to school today." Ruby covered her eyes with her hands to block out the daylight, which was aggravating her already pounding headache and laid back down on the sofa. Mandy burst into tears and ran back up to her bedroom. She hadn't seen her mum like this before. She took comfort in her dolls, playing with them for the next hour or so before going back down to see if her mum was up yet. She crept quietly into the lounge and found her mum still lying in the same position as when she left her.

Mandy was quite hungry by now so decided to get her own breakfast. She had never done it herself before but had watched her mum do it so knew what to do. She took a bowl from the cupboard and placed it on the table. The fridge freezer was too tall for Mandy so she dragged a chair over and climbed on it. She opened the fridge door and grabbed a glass milk bottle. Carefully she climbed down from the chair and had almost managed when she slipped and fell. The pint of milk fell from her hand and smashed onto the floor, milk and glass spilling everywhere. Mandy picked herself up and tried to reach the dishcloth, which was by the sink. She couldn't reach it so she went into the lounge to wake her mum up and tell her what had happened.

"Mummy I dropped the milk," said Mandy quietly as she gently nudged her mum. Ruby opened her eyes slowly and raised her head. She put her hands over her eyes as the throbbing in her head began.

"What now? Can't you see I'm asleep?" Ruby groaned.

"I didn't mean to Mummy, but I was hungry and you wouldn't wake up." Ruby sat up slowly, the throbbing in her head almost unbearable. She stood up slowly and made her way into the kitchen followed by her daughter.

"What the hell have you done? Look at the mess. I've got to clear that up now! Get out of my sight you stupid girl!" Mandy ran out of the back door into the garden. The tears were streaming down her little face. Mummy had never treated her like this before and she was becoming frightened. It wasn't long before Mandy started to feel the cold – she had run out of the house without putting her coat on. She didn't want to go back inside though, because she was afraid of what her mum would do, so she made for the shed at the back of the garden.

The shed door was a bit stiff but Mandy managed to pull it open. Inside to the right there was a shelf, which Derek had built for Ruby to use for planting seeds and cuttings. There were stacks and stacks of flowerpots on the shelf ready for the next season's gardening. On the left there was a row of long nails hammered into the wall, which Ruby used to prop up her fork, spade and other gardening tools. At the end of the row in the corner stood a lawn mower. At the back of the shed there was a small window, about 10 Inches Square. An overgrown Honeysuckle outside obstructed the limited light that it let in. Ruby was going to cut it back this year along with various other jobs she had planned for the garden. Underneath the window was an old fold-up garden seat. Mandy closed the door behind her and climbed onto the chair. She had stopped crying by now and rubbed away the remaining tearstains from her eyes. As she sat on the chair she looked around the shed. The corners were full of cobwebs and dried up leaves that had been blown in by the wind. The shelf was covered with compost and dirt that had spilled out of the various pots. Although it was perhaps one or two degrees warmer inside the shed Mandy was still shivering. She was also very hungry, as she didn't get her breakfast in the end. She decided to wait a few minutes and then go back indoors and see if Mummy was feeling better now.

As she walked back into the kitchen Mandy saw that her mum had cleaned up the mess on the floor. She went into the lounge where she saw Ruby sitting on the sofa with a cup of coffee in her hand. Nervously the little girl spoke.

"Can I have my breakfast now, Mummy? I'm sorry I made a mess before."

"Yes sweetie. Come on I'll make you some toast." Ruby stood up, still holding the coffee mug in her hand and walked out into the kitchen followed by her daughter. She put the mug down and turned to Mandy.

"Listen sweetie, I'm sorry I shouted at you earlier but I wasn't feeling too well. Let's just forget about it."

Mandy instantly forgave her mum. "Okay. Are we going out today?"

"No not today, but I've got to go to the corner shop so we can get you some sweeties there if you like." Ruby had realised that the last bottle of vodka was nearly empty. She was at the stage now where she couldn't go more than a couple of hours before needing a drink, although she still wouldn't admit to herself that she had a problem. She took a couple of aspirin while Mandy finished her toast and drink and then washed up the few dishes that were there. The two of them then walked to the corner shop hand in hand. Ruby knew the way she had spoken to her daughter that morning was out of order and felt awful about it, but it didn't stop her buying more vodka. Once back home Mandy took the sweets mum had bought her upstairs and set up a tea party for her dolls. Ruby meanwhile sat in the lounge to read a magazine she had bought. Almost subconsciously she had poured herself a vodka before sitting. More and more often she needed a drink before doing anything and managed to get through the rest of the day with the aid of the alcohol. Mandy was an easy child to look after and was quite content to play on her own. Ruby knew that she was neglecting her daughter but seemed unable to bring herself to do anything about it. She kept promising herself that she would stop drinking 'after this one' but never seemed able to fulfil that promise.

Over the course of the next few months Ruby's drinking became worse and worse. She would spend most of the days and nights lying on the sofa surrounded by empty vodka bottles and the remains of sandwiches and toast, which were the only meals she seemed to manage to make. Little Mandy spent more and more time playing on her own in her bedroom, and when Mummy was in a bad mood she would stay outside. She had worked out for herself that when the sun went in it was time to go to bed. When she did go indoors at the end of the day she would usually find Ruby asleep on the sofa. She had learned not to wake her up for fear of getting shouted at or hit.

Mandy stopped going to playschool in March that year. Ruby had made some excuse to the playschool leader about relatives looking after her while she went to work. Of course this was a lie, Ruby most of the time was either too drunk or too hung over to take her daughter to school. The school though, had no reason to think any different and so no questions were asked. Mandy wasn't due to start school full time until September that year.

Ruby had also fallen out with Joyce not long after Valentine's Day that year. Joyce had taken Mandy out for the afternoon and noticed that she had become very quiet and withdrawn. She tried to ask Mandy if there was a problem but the little girl was very loyal to her mother and wouldn't say what had been happening. Instead she just put up with her mother's worsening temper, keeping out of her way as much as possible. Joyce tried tactfully to talk to Ruby about her concerns for Mandy.

"Is she okay Ruby?" said Joyce as she dropped Mandy back home one afternoon.

"Why shouldn't she be?" Ruby snapped back. "What has she been saying about me?"

"Nothing, that's the problem. She just doesn't seem to be her usual happy self. Are you coping okay on your own? You know where we are if you need any help."

"I don't need your help," Ruby replied sharply. "In fact I don't need you sniffing round here anymore. Derek's dead and as far as I'm concerned it's just me and Mandy from now on. We don't need do-gooders like you around." Joyce was both shocked and upset at the way Ruby had spoken to her. She tried to calm her down but to no avail. Ruby closed the door in Joyce's face and told her never to come back again. Joyce cried as she drove back home to tell Viv what had just happened.

"I don't know what to do Viv. I'm sure something's wrong. Mandy is usually so happy. I do hope Ruby's not drinking."

"Leave it a couple of days and we'll both go round there together."

Chapter 4

Upstairs Mandy was playing with her dolls as the doorbell rang. Ruby was also upstairs, lying on her bed. She had managed to get upstairs the previous night before collapsing in a drunken state onto her bed.

"Shall I get it, Mummy?"

"No, I don't want to speak to anyone. Just leave it." Mandy looked out of her bedroom window, which faced the front of the house. From behind the net curtain she could just make out the faces of Nanny and Granfy. She ran to her mum's bedroom.

"Nanny's here! Can I let her in?"

"That's all I need," Ruby mumbled to herself. "Mandy, open your bedroom window and tell them I'm not well. They'll have to come back another day." It was too late. Mandy had already run downstairs and opened the front door.

"Hello my darling, how are you today?" asked Joyce as she hugged her.

"I'm fine thanks Nanny, but Mummy's not well. I think she's got another headache." Joyce gave a concerned glance back at Viv who was just coming through the door. Ruby meanwhile had heard the commotion and got up, putting her dressing gown on. She braced herself for the inquest that was surely to begin when she got downstairs.

"Hello Viv, Joyce," Ruby looked at them both in turn as she greeted them. "How about some coffee?" Joyce was too busy looking around at the state of the kitchen to hear Ruby. She couldn't believe her eyes. It was just like Christmas morning when she had come to pick Ruby up. The washing up hadn't been done for a number of days, the bin not emptied yet again, and there was a collection of empty bottles of cheap vodka on the worktop next to the sink.

"No wonder you don't want us around here anymore, worried we might find out what you've been up to," said Joyce as she pointed at the empty bottles.

"I don't need a lecture from you thank you very much. I told you the other day I don't want you around here anymore. Why can't you just mind your own business?"

"Now, now, let's just calm down," Viv butted in realising that Mandy was in the room. "Mandy, why don't you go upstairs and play and I'll be up in a minute." He smiled at the little girl as she obeyed and headed for upstairs. As soon as the bedroom door closed upstairs Joyce started again.

"I think Mandy should come and stay with us. You can't possibly look after her in the state you're in."

"And I think you had better leave before I throw you out." Ruby was seething with rage at the mere suggestion of her daughter staying with her grandparents. "What gives you the right to come round here and tell me what's best for my child? She's nothing to do with you anymore. Now get out and don't you ever come back."

Viv and Joyce both got up to leave.

"If that's how you want it Ruby that's fine, but don't think you've heard the last of us. I'll be phoning the Social Services as soon as I get home. You're a drunk, you're not even fit to look after yourself let alone a four year old daughter."

"Just get lost!" replied Ruby as she slammed the door shut behind her in-laws. She turned and lent with her back against the door just long enough to get her breath back. She heard the noise of Joyce's car engine speeding off up the road and headed for the stairs.

Mandy was still playing quietly with her dolls when her mother burst through the bedroom door.

"You stupid little bitch! Why did you let them in?" The doll fell from Mandy's hand as her mother's hand struck her around the face. She screamed as she put her own little hand where her mother's had struck.

"I'm sorry Mummy, I didn't hear you," replied Mandy, shaking with fright.

"Don't lie to me, you heard me alright, you just wanted to see good old Nanny. Well I've got news for you, you won't be seeing Nanny ever again." By now Mandy was sobbing her eyes out. She wished Daddy hadn't died; Mummy never hit her when Daddy was here.

"And you can stop that stupid noise unless you really want something to cry for." Ruby stormed out of the room and downstairs to pour herself a fresh vodka. Meanwhile Mandy laid herself on her bed and cried herself to sleep. She woke a couple of hours later, by now early evening and crept downstairs to see where her mum was. She pushed open the lounge door just enough to get her head through and saw Ruby lying asleep on the sofa. The glass she had previously been holding had fallen out of her hand, spilling what was left of the drink onto the carpet in front of her. Mandy went into the kitchen to see if there were any biscuits for her to eat. She looked in the biscuit tin but it was empty. She pulled a chair over to the worktop in order to see if she could find anything else. All she could see was an opened loaf of bread so she took a slice from the packet. She didn't notice the spots of mould as she took a bite from the slice. She thought it tasted a bit funny but was so hungry she ate it anyway, after all it seemed that there was nothing else to eat. It had been a few weeks now since Ruby had cooked her daughter a proper meal; biscuits and toast seemed to be the norm most days. Mandy was too young to know any different. She washed the bread down with water from the tap and went upstairs to her bedroom. There she stayed until it was dark and put herself into bed, knowing that Mummy probably wouldn't come up to say goodnight to her.

The next morning Ruby received a telephone call.

"Hello, could I please speak to Mrs Ruby Croft?"

"Yes, speaking." This was the phone call Ruby had been half-expecting. Why couldn't Joyce just mind her own business?

"My name is Fran Howard and I work for the Social Services. Would you mind if I made an appointment to come and see you and your daughter at home?"

"Why do you need to come and see me, have I done something wrong?" Ruby knew exactly what it was all about but wasn't going to let on.

"We've received some information and need to visit just so that we can see for ourselves if there is any cause for concern."

"Okay if you think you need to, I have nothing to hide. When would you like to come?"

"This afternoon if that's alright with you."

"Yes of course, what time?" Ruby didn't let the panic show in her voice. She agreed 2 o'clock would be fine and replaced the receiver. She sat on the sofa to gather her thoughts and looked at the clock. 9.15 a.m. She had the whole morning to sort the house out.

"Mandy, come down here," she shouted to her daughter who had not yet come downstairs. She had been awake but had heard her mum downstairs and had decided to stay out of the way after yesterday's events.

"Yes Mummy?" she said as she entered the lounge.

"We've got some work to do today. There's a lady coming to see us this afternoon and she wants to know if we are coping on our own. This house has got to spotless, so we'll have breakfast and then get started." Ruby went into the kitchen followed by Mandy and looked in the cupboard to find some cereal. The cupboard was empty. It was the first time in days that Ruby had actually looked in the cupboards; it was also the first time for days that she had been sober. It suddenly dawned on Ruby just how badly she had treated Mandy. She turned to her as she spoke softly.

"Mandy sweetheart, I'm so sorry. You must think I'm such a bad mother. I'll make it up to you, I promise. I've been so selfish and haven't thought about you at all. Come on, we'll go to the café and get a big breakfast. Then we'll go to the supermarket and buy all your favourite food. How about I get some mince and make us spaghetti Bolognese tonight? Then we can have some ice-cream for afters."

"Can we have chocolate ice-cream?" asked Mandy, jumping up and down with excitement.

"You can have anything you want sweetheart." Ruby didn't deserve such a loving, forgiving daughter. She had put her through hell the past few weeks and it was all forgotten in an instant. "Come on, let's go now," she continued, "we'll sort the house out when we get back." So the two of them enjoyed breakfast at the café together and then went to the local supermarket to stock up on groceries. Once back home Mandy helped her mother tidy up the house. It took a good couple of hours. All the empty vodka bottles were put into a large black bin-liner and put outside in the dustbin, the dishes were washed and dried up, glasses were put back on the mini-bar and the lounge carpet vacuumed. Ruby really needed a drink but managed to go without. She couldn't afford to let the Social Worker think there may be a problem. She was also worried about what Mandy might possibly say.

"Mandy sweetheart, you are happy living here with me, aren't you?"

53

"Yes Mummy, but I don't like it when you shout at me or hit me." Ruby felt so guilty. She knelt down so as to be at her daughter's height.

"You mustn't say anything to the lady about me hitting you, sweetheart. You know I didn't mean to don't you, and I promise I will never ever do it again. If the lady finds out she'll send you away and you won't be able to see me again."

"I don't want to be sent away Mummy. I won't say anything." They finished tidying up the house and had just enough time for a drink before the doorbell rang.

"Mrs Croft?" asked the woman standing at the door with a brief case in her hand. She must have been in her late fifties, with grey-white hair tied back into a bun. She wore small round spectacles, which Ruby thought made her look more like a schoolteacher than a Social Worker.

"Please come in," invited Ruby as she beckoned the visitor in. She led her into the lounge where Mandy was already sitting in the chair.

"Hello young lady, you must be Mandy." The Social Worker smiled as she sat herself down on the sofa. "My name is Fran and I've come to see how you and your Mummy are getting on. Would you mind awfully if I spoke to Mummy on her own for a few minutes?"

"Go and play in your room for a while, sweetheart. I'll call you down when we've finished." Mandy did as her mum asked and took herself upstairs. Fran Howard turned towards Ruby.

"Mrs Croft, I'm here as part of my duty on behalf of the Social Services department. We've had some information with regard to the welfare of Mandy."

"What sort of information? And who from?"

"I'm sorry Mrs Croft but I'm not allowed to say where our information comes from, but you must understand that we have to check out every home where there may be possible problems."

Ruby knew exactly what information and who it was from but there was no way that she was going to give anything away.

"Yes of course. You wouldn't be doing your job if you didn't, but it seems a shame to waste your time when there is no problem. Mandy and I are managing okay since my husband died last November. It was hard at first but we've come through the worst of it. We both still miss him very much but we have each other and have become closer now than when Derek was alive. I can't believe that somebody has phoned you saying that we're not managing."

"Actually we were told that you may have a drink problem and that Mandy isn't being fed properly." Fran Howard looked straight into Ruby's eyes as she spoke.

"Me with a drink problem!" Ruby put on a surprised expression. "But I never touch the stuff!" She pointed to the mini-bar. "Everything you see over there is from when Derek was alive. We used to have a lot of dinner parties. I've been saying for ages that I should get rid of that bar. I wish I had now, and then maybe I wouldn't be accused of having a drink problem. As for Mandy not being fed, you can go and check the fridge and kitchen cupboards if you like…"

"We'll get round to that in due course, Mrs Croft," the older woman interrupted. "Like I said before we do have to check things out for ourselves."

"Yes I understand," replied Ruby. "Would you like to have a look around? I've nothing to hide."

"Yes please," answered Fran Howard. "Could we start in the kitchen?" The two women went into the kitchen where the Social Worker looked in all the cupboards. She was quite satisfied with the amount of groceries that she found. She was also looking around for any evidence of Ruby's possible drinking but could find none.

"Looking at the healthy state of these cupboards I can't see any signs that you aren't feeding your daughter, Mrs Croft. Would you mind if I went upstairs to talk to Mandy on her own?"

"No, of course I don't mind. Her room is the first on the right." Ruby was worried about what Mandy might say but didn't let it show. She sat in the lounge while she waited. It was only about ten minutes but seemed a lot longer to Ruby. She feared the worst. To be up there this long Mandy must have said something. Ruby's heart began racing as Mandy came downstairs followed by the Social Worker.

"Everything all right?" asked Ruby as confidently as she could.

"Yes Mrs Croft. As far as I'm concerned there is no problem here. You have a very bright, happy child and you should be very proud of her." Ruby couldn't believe the relief she felt at that moment.

"Does that mean you won't be coming here anymore?" asked Ruby.

"I don't see any reason why we should, but if you have any worries you know where we are. It's not easy bringing up a child on your own but you seem to be managing very well." Fran Howard headed for the front door. "I'll write out a report when I get back to the office to say that the case is now closed." They said their goodbyes and Ruby closed the door.

"I don't know what you said up there, sweetheart but it worked."

"I just said that I am very happy living here with you and I told her we went out for a big breakfast today."

"I'm very proud of you, Mandy. Why don't you go and play. It will soon be tea time and don't forget I'm making your favourite tonight." Ruby filled the kettle to make herself a cup of coffee. For the first time in weeks she felt good. She also realised that she had just had a very narrow escape. She promised herself that she would stop drinking and take more care of her daughter.

Chapter 5

Within a week Ruby was drinking again, only this time more than ever. Mandy quickly learned to stay out of her mother's way. More and more often Ruby hit her for no apparent reason. At four years old Mandy just came to accept it as part of normal life- there was no-one around to tell her any different. Now she didn't have Nanny or Granfy, and within a couple of weeks she had stopped attending playschool.

It wasn't long before the cupboards were once again bare. Ruby bought the odd loaf of bread and packet of biscuits when she went to the shop to buy her supply of vodka, and this was basically all Mandy ate for the next few months. Mandy soon came to realise that if she didn't want to go hungry she would have to save her food, so every time her mum brought bread or biscuits she would sneak some out into the shed. She had found an old sandwich box in the cupboard and used this to keep the food fresh.

Ruby did have the odd 'good' day when she would treat Mandy. They would go out to the park, or to feed the ducks by the river. On these days she would usually go food shopping to stock up. Mandy loved it when they went shopping because she could stock up on her secret supply in the shed. So this is how life went on for the rest of the summer. Mandy became very lonely; apart from her mum she never spoke to anyone else. She did ask her mum on the odd occasion if she could see Nanny and Granfy, but was told that they didn't want to see her anymore. Mandy was very upset by this and couldn't understand it. She thought it was her fault, perhaps she had said something wrong the last time she saw them. She had to be careful when she spoke about Nanny and Granfy – if she said anything at the wrong time she would get a mouthful of abuse from her mother.

Little Mandy was really looking forward to starting school in September, at least then she would have some friends to talk to. Ruby had managed to take her out on one of her 'sober' days and buy her a brand new uniform. Although Mandy was excited about her new uniform, Ruby had spoiled her joy by constantly telling her how much it had cost her, and that if she so much as put a scratch on her new shoes she would make her go to school in bare feet.

Another problem began for Mandy that summer in 1973. She had just suffered one of her mum's 'bad' days. All day long she had been shouted at for no apparent reason.

"You're always in my way. Why can't you just stay out of my sight?" All Mandy had done was come in from outside to get herself a drink of water. Ruby was in the kitchen trying to light a cigarette (another recent habit that she had taken up). She had broken two matches and took out her frustration on Mandy, who had walked in just at the wrong time.

"I only want a drink, Mummy," said Mandy as she took a glass from the worktop.

"Don't you answer me back, young lady," shouted Ruby as she snatched the glass from her daughter's hand and smashed it into the sink. Mandy ran out into the garden before her mum had a chance to do anything else to her. She stayed outside for a couple of hours to let her mum calm down. When she went back indoors she found her as usual asleep on the sofa, with a half empty glass on the coffee table next to her. Mandy thought better of trying to wake her up and went to the kitchen. She made herself a 'meal' of biscuits and crisps before going up to her bedroom. Here she stayed for the rest of the day until it was dark outside and once again put herself to bed. The next morning when she woke up she felt cold. Then she realised that it wasn't cold she felt, but damp. She had wet her bed.

Mandy started to cry because she knew that Mummy would be very cross, so she decided not to tell her. Instead she just put the covers back over as best she could and took off her nightdress. She hung it over the chair next to the bed thinking that it would be dry by the time she went back to bed that night. Mandy got herself dressed and managed to get through the rest of the day without upsetting her mum too much, which was getting more and more difficult to do lately. Ruby was in a fairly good mood as she had walked up to the shop and stocked up on her vodka supply. Mandy spent most of the day outside until Ruby called her in for dinner. She must have been in a good mood because she had managed to make beans on toast! At the back of her mind Mandy wondered whether she should tell her mum about her little 'accident' in the night. She plucked up the courage and began to speak.

"Mummy," she said quietly.

"Yes sweetheart, what is it?"

"Please don't be cross with me."

"Why, what have you done?" Ruby's attitude was already changing for the worse.

"When I woke up today my sheet was wet." Mandy was not expecting what happened next.

"You dirty little bitch! What are you, a baby?"

"I, I'm sorry Mummy, I didn't mean to." She started crying and began shaking.

"Get out of my sight you stupid girl." Mandy headed for the door and turned to her mum.

"What shall I do with the sheet Mummy?"

"You'll just have to sleep in it, won't you? I haven't got time to clean up after your mess." Ruby walked out of the kitchen, past Mandy and into the lounge to pour herself a drink. As she got close to Mandy the little girl flinched, as if expecting her mother to hit her.

"Don't worry, I'm not going to hit you, just go to your room and don't come back downstairs." Ruby slammed the lounge door behind her, leaving Mandy in the kitchen doorway, sobbing her heart out. She went upstairs and took off her clothes, putting the urine-stained nightdress from the night before back on. She then got into bed, the sheet still slightly damp. She moved to the edge of the bed, where she found a dry patch, curled herself into a ball and cried herself to sleep.

The next morning Mandy found herself once again lying in a wet bed. She knew she couldn't tell her mum so she just put the covers over and didn't say anything. She had gone downstairs for breakfast when Ruby walked into the kitchen, lit herself a cigarette, poured herself a vodka from a half-empty bottle on the worktop, and went back upstairs. This is how the next few weeks went on. Ruby barely spoke to Mandy, and when she did it was just to moan at her or tell her off for something unimportant. She had been that drunk that she didn't even notice the worsening smell of urine that was wafting through the house. Mandy had wet every night since that first time and had taken the sheet off the bed some days ago. She had stuffed it behind the chest of drawers to hide it, and was now sleeping on the bare mattress with just her dressing gown over her. There was a dry blanket but Mandy used this to cover the bed in the mornings, hiding the wet mattress underneath.

A few days before Mandy was due to start school full-time, Ruby realised that she would have to start getting into the routine of taking her daughter to school every morning and picking her up again in the afternoon. This wasn't going to be easy. She would have to cut down on the drinking. It took her a couple of days and a lot of coffee, but she managed to get herself sober enough to sort everything ready for school. She had even managed to bring herself round to talking to her daughter properly and decided on this particular evening to get her school uniform ready.

"Mandy, let's go up and try your uniform to make sure you've got everything you need." Ruby started to climb the stairs and Mandy followed. This was the moment the young girl was dreading. Mummy was sure to see her bed.

"What the hell has been going on in here?" Ruby was almost screaming at her daughter, her face red with rage. "It stinks of piss in here." She pulled back the blanket to reveal the bare urine-soaked mattress. The outer material of the mattress had almost worn away where the acid from the urine had soaked in. By now Mandy was stood right behind her mother who reached back and grabbed her by her hair. Still holding her hair she pulled her towards the edge of the bed. From here Ruby pushed her daughter's head forward and rubbed her face in the urine-soaked mattress.

Mandy held her breathe as she struggled to escape her mother's grip, but it was no good. What comparison is there between a defenceless five-year-old and an angry, alcohol-fuelled adult temper? As she held her, Ruby put her own face close to Mandy's.

"You're a disgusting, stinking little bitch. Only babies piss the bed. Look at the state of this mattress. You can't sleep on that now, can you?" With this Ruby pulled her daughter, still by the hair and threw her onto the floor. Mandy crawled into the corner of the room, snivelling and cowering like a frightened animal. She watched while her mother, still in a frightening rage, dragged the mattress from the bed base and through the landing to the top of the stairs. She then pushed the mattress, letting it fall to the bottom, rebounding first off one side of the stairs and then the other. Ruby followed the mattress, picking it up from the bottom of the stairs and dragged it through the kitchen, leaving it just outside the back door. She slammed the back door shut and returned upstairs, where Mandy was still crouched in the corner.

"You've ruined the mattress so you'll have to sleep on that now," said Ruby, pointing to the bed base. "I can't afford to buy a new bed, and there's no point anyway if you're going to piss in it every night." Ruby opened the wardrobe door to take out the uniform hanging up inside.

"Come here and try this on." Mandy quickly got up and did as she was told. She was trying her hardest to stop crying, letting out a sniffle every now and then. Ruby checked the uniform was okay and told her daughter to take it off.

"You stink. You'll have to have a bath," said Ruby as she went into the bathroom and turned on the hot tap. She sat on the edge of the bath while it filled with water. She then turned off the taps without checking the temperature of the water.

"Get in, Stinky," ordered Ruby to her daughter. Mandy put her foot into the water and quickly pulled it out again.

"It's too hot, Mummy."

"I said get in!"

"But it's too hot," Mandy protested. She couldn't believe what happened next. The little girl screamed as her mum picked her up and placed her in the scolding water. Mandy managed to put her feet down and get herself into a standing position. The pain was unbearable; it was as if the skin was being peeled from her feet right the way up her shins.

"Sit down!"

"I can't Mummy, it's burning." Mandy was screaming in agony by now.

"I said sit down," commanded Ruby as she pushed down on Mandy's shoulders, forcing her into the water.

"No Mummy please. It's burning me." Mandy was crying uncontrollably as the top of her legs and the rest of her body up to her waistline came into contact with the water.

"It's your own fault. If you weren't such a dirty bitch you wouldn't need a bath, would you?" Ruby showed no sign of regard as to what she was doing to her daughter. It was almost as if an evil spirit had taken over her, telling her to do these awful things. She picked up the flannel, which was hanging over the edge of the bath and rinsed it in the water. She winced a little as the water burned her own hand slightly, but still she carried on, rubbing the hot flannel over Mandy's body. The little girl screamed with every drop of water that poured down her back.

"Pull the plug out," ordered Ruby as she picked up a towel from the radiator. Mandy pulled out the plug and stood up, her little body red-raw from the scolding water. Ruby grabbed her tightly around the waist and lifted her up, placing her down heavily on the floor. She put a towel around her and rubbed her all over, roughly. This just made her already raw skin burn even more. Mandy began to feel dizzy, her vision blurring. Without warning she collapsed, Ruby just catching her before she fell to the floor in a heap.

"Oh my God, what have I done?" said Ruby to herself as she carried her daughter into her own bedroom and onto her bed. As she was laid onto the bed Mandy woke up.

"It's okay sweetie, just lie down." Ruby had in an instant changed from an evil, tortuous creature to the caring mother that up until a year ago Mandy had always known.

"Mummy I'm sorry about the bed. I didn't mean to wet," Mandy said as she began to cry again. Ruby held her hand as she sat on the edge of the bed.

"Listen sweetie, it's me that should be sorry. I don't know what's happened to me lately but I know I shout at you more than I should. I just can't help it. I'll make it up to you. I know I've said that to you before but this time I mean it. Why don't you get into bed, you can sleep in my bed tonight, and I'll go downstairs and make you some warm milk." Mandy did as she was told while Ruby went downstairs. She returned five minutes later with two mugs, one full of coffee for herself and the other with warm milk for her daughter. The two of them sat up in bed, talking about school and how Mandy would have lots of new friends to play with. Mandy was getting tired and so once they had finished their drinks Ruby put the mugs on the bedside table and switched off the light. It wasn't long before they were both asleep, Mandy held close in her mother's arms.

Chapter 6

Ruby managed to refrain from drinking for the next few days. The realisation of what she had done to her daughter had set in. Luckily Mandy's delicate skin had tolerated the scorching water and hadn't left any marks. While she was sober for these few days Ruby opened some of the mail, which had been piling up on the floor in front of the letterbox. There was a cut off notice from the phone company and a letter from the housing department of the local council warning of legal action if she did not contact them about the 'substantial' amount of rent arrears. There were also letters from the gas and electric companies asking for payment within the next seven days to avoid further action being taken.

Among the pile of letters was one from the bank. This was the most worrying one of all. She hadn't realised just how much of her money she had wasted away on her ever-worsening alcohol addiction. When Derek died Ruby was left a fairly healthy bank balance from the life insurance he had taken out. She had also received around £2000 from the oil company in compensation for the accident. She could have fought for a lot more but at the time she was in still in shock over Derek's sudden death and so just accepted the first offer of payment. The letter from the bank accompanied a monthly statement, which showed a balance plummeting swiftly into the red. It also advised her that she could no longer use her credit card, as she hadn't been keeping up with payments.

Although Ruby was sorely tempted to drink again at this point she was still feeling guilty about the bath episode and managed not to succumb. Instead she put her efforts into making sure that Mandy was okay She moved the bed base that was left in Mandy's room and replaced it with a 'put you up' bed, which in the past had been used for occasional visitors. The next couple of days were more like the old times that Mandy loved so much, they went to the park and to the local river where they fed the ducks. When they weren't out they stayed in and watched the television together. Mandy also had stopped wetting the bed for these last few days.

It seemed like no time until the morning came for Mandy's first day at school. She was up and raring to go by about seven that morning.

"Come on Mummy, wake up," she said excitedly as she tugged at her mum's arm.

"Okay, okay, I'm coming. Just give me a minute." Ruby sat up slowly and looked at the clock on the bedside table. Mandy ran downstairs and sat at the kitchen table waiting for mum to make her breakfast. It wasn't long before Ruby came down and put the kettle on. She needed a coffee and a cigarette before she could do anything. Really she wanted a vodka, the craving still strong even after a few days, but had forced herself to resist the temptation. Ruby poured some cereal and milk into a bowl and put it on the table in front of her daughter.

"All set then, sweetheart?" she asked as Mandy quickly ate her breakfast.

"Yep, is it time to go yet?"

"No, there's still an hour before we have to go. What would you like in your sandwiches today? Now let me guess, it wouldn't be chocolate spread by any chance would it?"

"How did you know, Mummy?"

"Because I'm clever," smiled Ruby as she made the sandwiches and put them in Mandy's lunchbox along with a packet of crisps and a chocolate bar. She then poured some orange squash into a flask. She put both the flask and lunchbox into Mandy's brand new school bag.

"Why don't you go upstairs and play while I just wash up the breakfast things. I'll call you when it's time to go."

"Okay Mummy." Mandy answered and ran upstairs as she was told. Ruby washed up and sat down at the table with a fresh cup of coffee. She really did need a drink; it was getting harder all the time to manage without.

Soon it was time to go. The sight of her daughter in her brand new uniform on her first day of school brought tears to Ruby's eyes. Derek would have been so proud of her as indeed she was. They walked down the road hand in hand, past the corner shop and up to the main road. Once across the zebra crossing the school was just around the corner. Mandy was getting nervous now, there were so many children and she didn't know any of them.

"Don't be worried sweetie, you'll soon make friends." Ruby led her through the school gates and across the playground to where a group of teachers were congregated. The school bell rang and everything went quiet, anxious children holding on to their parents' hands for comfort. One of the teachers began calling out instructions. She introduced each teacher in turn and asked the children to stand in a line behind their allocated teacher. She called out the first two names and two lines of children began to line up behind them. Then she called out the third name.

"Could all children going into Mrs Albright's class please line up."

"This is you sweetie," said Ruby as she knelt down to give her daughter a kiss, "have a lovely day and don't you worry about anything." Ruby walked back a few paces and watched as the line of children was led into the school. Already Mandy was talking to another little girl who looked just as nervous as she did. She was so busy talking that she didn't even turn back to say goodbye to her mother, who, along with most of the other mums was fighting the tears in her eyes and lump in her throat. Ruby headed back home. While walking back she began thinking about how quickly time had passed, it seemed like only yesterday when she and Derek were walking around pushing their baby daughter in her pram. She remembered the first time she had sat up, and then crawled. Then just after her first birthday she took her first wobbly steps. Ruby had been holding her in a standing position while Derek kneeled in front of her, beckoning her to come towards him. Then she did it; first one step, then another before she stumbled into her dad's arms. Both parent's had clapped and cheered their baby daughter, they were the proudest mum and dad in the world that day. Ruby's eyes watered as she remembered those good days. Why did life have to be so cruel? Why did he have to die? This was the question Ruby had asked herself so often while drinking herself to sleep. If he hadn't died then she wouldn't have started drinking. If she hadn't started drinking then she wouldn't have been so cruel to Mandy.

She arrived back home. It was now that she realised she would be on her own for most of the days. What was she going to do? She decided to get stuck into the house; it had got into a bit of a state lately and would keep her occupied for at least the next few days. So Ruby spent the rest of Mandy's first day at school washing, scrubbing, ironing and dusting. The time went fairly quickly and she was proud of herself for managing to get through the day without touching a drop of vodka. Soon it was 3 o'clock and time to walk the short distance to pick Mandy up. When she arrived Ruby waited with all the other mothers, each one anxious to hear about their own child's first day at school. The bell rang, and within a minute or so the doors opened and a steady stream of children came out to meet their patents. By the looks of it the day had gone well; unlike the neatly tucked in uniforms, newly brushed and pony-tailed hair, and quiet, shy children from first thing that morning, there were happy, smiling faces, all of them seemed to have found their voices again.

Ruby soon spotted her daughter running towards her, arms held out ready to hug her mum.

71

"Mummy, look what I did for you!" In her hand was a large piece of paper, filled with brightly coloured splodges of paint.

"Wow, look at that!" said Ruby as she took the painting. "We'll have to hang it up on the wall." The two of them walked back home, Mandy skipping happily alongside her mother as she told her all about her activities that day.

When they reached home Ruby made a coffee for herself and some squash for her daughter. Then Mandy went upstairs, took off her uniform and folded it neatly on the chair before putting on her usual clothes. She stayed upstairs and played for an hour or so with Katy and the rest of her dolls. She lined them up and pretended they were in a classroom and that she was their teacher. Meanwhile downstairs Ruby prepared dinner. She was so glad that Mandy had enjoyed her first day at school. She called her down as she put the meal on the table and they ate together, talking about how the day had gone.

The first week of school went without any problems. Mandy had made some new friends and Ruby had managed to stay away from the vodka and keep her mind on getting the house straight and keeping up with the chores. This changed though, when on the following Monday after getting back from taking Mandy from school there was a knock on the door.

"Mrs Croft?"

"Yes." Replied Ruby to the official looking man stood in the doorway.

"I'm from the council housing department and I'm afraid I have to give you this." He handed Ruby an envelope.

"What is it?" she asked although in the back of her mind she already knew the answer to that question.

"It's a court summons. The council want to retake possession of this house because you've not paid the rent or taken any steps to clear the arrears that have amounted."

"But they can't take this house. Where will I live? I have a young daughter."

"I'm sorry Mrs Croft, it's out of our hands now, and it's up to the court to decide what happens now. We've given you plenty of warnings and chances to sort this out, but you've just ignored any correspondence we've sent you."

"I've just got a bit behind, that's all. There's no need for court action. I'll phone the bank and get a loan and then I can pay what I owe." Ruby was struggling to say the right thing to get the council official to stop any court action but she could see that nothing was going to change his mind.
"If you pay the full amount owing before the court date then there'll be no problem, we can stop the proceedings, but until then there's nothing I can do. Good day, Mrs Croft."

The man walked away before Ruby had a chance to say any more. She closed the door and took a deep breath. What was she going to do? She knew that the bank wouldn't help, her debt with them was becoming out of control. She would have to claim benefit, something that she hadn't done up to now; Derek had always worked and provided for her and Mandy. Ruby hadn't realised just how little money she had– she hadn't checked the bank balance since Derek died, she just assumed that he had left enough for her to live on. She went back into the kitchen and lit a cigarette. She thought about pouring herself a vodka and found it very difficult to resist, but instead she made a cup of coffee. She managed to get through the rest of the day's housework without giving in, lighting up a cigarette or making coffee every time she thought about having something stronger.

Mandy was as cheerful as ever when she came out of school. She had been given a merit point for writing neatly and was so proud of herself.

"Mummy can we stop at the shop and buy some sweeties?"

"Yes but not too many, I haven't got much money in my purse." It was the first time that Ruby had ever told her daughter that; money had never been an issue. Now she was going to have to watch every penny she spent. They entered the corner shop and Mandy chose her sweets and gave them to her mum. Ruby picked up a pint of milk and took it to the counter with the sweets. While waiting for the customer in front of them to pack his groceries into a bag Ruby looked at the display of alcohol. The temptation was too great and she ended up going home with a bottle of vodka. So much for her having to watch the purse strings. They had dinner about 5 o'clock, after which Mandy went up for a bath. She then played in her room for an hour but was so tired after her busy day at school that she decided to go to bed early. Ruby tucked her daughter in and gave her a goodnight kiss. Within minutes the young girl was asleep.

Ruby washed up the dinner plates and filled the kettle to make some coffee. She began to think about money and how she was going to get out of the mess she was in financially. She just didn't have a clue what she was going to do; Derek had always dealt with money matters. The kettle boiled and switched itself off but Ruby ignored it. Instead she went into the lounge and over to the mini bar where she had put the new vodka bottle. She took a glass and placed it on top of the bar while she unscrewed the top of the bottle. She knew it was wrong but still she poured the liquid into the glass and then carried it and the bottle over to the coffee table before sitting. Ruby took the glass in her hand and held it up to her face, looking at the clear liquid as if inspecting it. She studied her distorted reflection in the glass, slowly twisting it in her hand. Then she took a sip. Within seconds the effects of the alcohol were starting to work, the problems of the day ebbing away as she took another sip. It tasted so good that Ruby finished the glass straight away before pouring herself another. All the efforts of the last couple of weeks had gone to waste and once again alcohol had taken over her life. History had repeated itself and within a couple of hours Ruby had drunk herself to sleep, not managing to take herself upstairs to bed, instead spending the night laid on the sofa, barely conscious.

Chapter 7

Mandy was awake early the next morning and quickly put on her uniform before going into her mum's bedroom to wake her up. She was surprised to find her not there and called down the stairs.

"Mummy, are you making breakfast?" There was no answer so Mandy went down the stairs. She looked in the kitchen but there was no sign of her mum, so she went into the lounge. She began to feel nervous, by now she knew the signs only too well. She crept over to where her mum was lying on the sofa and spoke softly.

"Mummy, it's time to get up now." Ruby was in such a deep sleep that she didn't even move, so Mandy spoke a bit louder, nudging her mum's arm as she did so.

"Mummy, wake up." Ruby stirred, opening her eyes slowly.

"Go away, I'm tired."

"But I've got to go to school, I'll be late," replied Mandy, moving away from her mother in case she lashed out.

"Damn bloody school," said Ruby as she sat up slowly, her head pounding, "Go and get some breakfast, I'll be up in a minute." Mandy did as she was asked and went into the kitchen. She made some cereal and had almost finished eating it when her mum entered the kitchen. Without speaking Ruby made herself a cup of coffee. She sat at the table, ignoring her daughter and lit a cigarette. The two of them sat in silence, Mandy too scared to say anything. She had seen her mum in this mood too many times.

Ruby looked at the clock, it was time to go.

"You ready then?" she asked.

"Yes but you haven't made my lunch yet," answered Mandy.

"We'll get something at the shop on the way, I'm not making sandwiches now, it's too late." Ruby picked up her purse as they both left the house. They walked as far as the corner shop in silence and went in. Ruby picked up a packet of crisps, an apple and a chocolate bar along with a carton of blackcurrant. She paid for them and told Mandy to put them in her school bag. Once out of the shop Ruby turned to her daughter.

"You can walk on your own from here, it's not far." Mandy looked worried.

"But I'm too little to walk on my own, Mummy, I might get lost."

"Don't be silly, of course you won't. Just do as you're told, I don't need this aggravation first thing in the morning." Ruby left the five-year-old standing as she turned and headed back down the street. All she wanted to do was get back and pour herself a drink. Mandy stood for a minute in disbelief, Mummy had just left her on her own! She looked in the direction of the school and saw some children walking with their parents. She walked quickly until she was just behind them and followed them closely across the zebra crossing and in to school.

Meanwhile, Ruby reached home and headed straight for the mini-bar; right now she needed a drink. Not long after she had finished the glass of vodka the doorbell rang. Ruby chose to ignore it and poured herself another glass. As she did the doorbell rang again. She cursed to herself and put down the glass then headed for the door.

"Hello Ruby."

"Joyce. What the hell do you want?"

"I've come to see if you and Mandy are okay it's been quite a while now and I thought maybe you've had a chance to calm down so that we can talk."

"You've got a bloody nerve. It was you who called the Social Services, trying to get Mandy taken away from me. Well I've got news for you, they couldn't find anything wrong, so why don't you do as I told you the last time I saw you and piss off!" Ruby was seething with rage by now.

"There's no need to be like that, Ruby. I was just concerned about Mandy."

"Well you've no need to be concerned. We're managing perfectly well and don't need any interference from the likes of you. Now get off my property before I throw you off." Ruby grabbed Joyce's arm and pushed her, almost knocking her off-balance.

"Is this how you treat Mandy, threatening her if she says of does something you don't like? Or is it just when you've had a drink? I take it you're still drinking?"

Ruby was at boiling point. She moved close to Joyce, pointing her finger right in the older woman's face, and spoke quietly but threateningly.

"What I do in my own house and with my own daughter is nothing to do with you or anyone else for that matter. Now get out of my sight."

"Don't worry I'm going, but there's obviously something not right here and I'm going to find out exactly what it is." Joyce walked away without saying anymore. It wasn't going to be easy but she was determined to find out exactly what was going on.

Ruby closed the door, still shaking with rage; how dare that woman come around after calling Social Services, she thought to herself. She entered the lounge, picking up the glass she had previously been holding and gulped the vodka down in one go. She poured herself another then lit a cigarette. This is how Ruby spent the rest of the day, eventually collapsing in a drunken stupor by mid-afternoon.

At school Mandy and her friends were packing away the paints and paper they had used for their art lesson.

"Hurry up children, its nearly time for the bell," said Mrs Albright as she laid out all the newly painted masterpieces to dry. Within ten minutes the children were all sat around their tables, coats on ready to go. The bell rang and the children rushed out to meet their parents. Mandy was the last to leave the classroom; she was worried about what sort of mood Mummy would be in after this morning. She walked out into the playground and over to the spot where her mum usually picked her up. Where was she? There was no sign of her.

Mandy watched as the playground slowly emptied, leaving her on her own. Mummy wasn't coming.

From the classroom, Mrs Albright could see the playground and noticed Mandy on her own. She quickly made her way outside to where the young girl was waiting.

"Mandy darling, is Mummy not here yet?"

"I think she's forgotten to pick me up," answered Mandy, almost crying.

"Don't worry, I'm sure she's just been delayed. She'll be here soon. Why don't you come and wait at the office, it's safer in there." Mandy followed the teacher to an area just outside the office where there was a row of chairs.

"You just wait here and I'll go into the office and telephone Mummy. I won't be a minute." Mrs Albright disappeared into the office to find Ruby's telephone number. She picked up the phone and dialled. At the other end of the line there was just a continuous tone. The phone line had been cut off. The teacher came back out to where Mandy was sitting patiently.

"I'm afraid I can't get hold of Mummy, so we'll give it another ten minutes or so. If she doesn't show up by then I'll give you a lift home. I have to go that way to get to my own house." Ten minutes passed and still no sign, so Mandy was given a lift home in her teacher's car. They pulled up outside the house.

"Here we are then, home at last," said Mrs Albright as she opened the door on Mandy's side of the car. They walked up the pathway and the teacher rang the doorbell. No answer. She tried again, keeping her finger on the button much longer this time. Still no answer. She looked over to the front window but the curtains were closed. She stood and thought for a moment. Then she took out a scrap of paper and a pen from her handbag and started to scribble a note to Ruby. She pushed the piece of paper through the letterbox and turned to Mandy.

"Well there doesn't seem to be any sign of Mummy. I've got your Nanny's address written down here so I think it's probably best if I drop you off there. I've written a note to Mummy so she knows what's going on. Come on, let's get back in the car." Mandy followed, worried about where her mum might be, but happy that she was going to see Nanny and Granfy. The little girl began chatting on the journey to her grandparents' house.

"I hope Nanny's pleased to see me." Mrs Albright thought it a rather odd thing for a five year old to say.

"Of course she will be, Nannies are always pleased to see their granddaughters."

"I haven't seen her for a long time, Mummy said that she doesn't want to see me anymore."

"Why wouldn't she want to see you, Mandy?"

"I don't know," answered Mandy, "I heard them arguing and then Mummy told Nanny to go. After that Mummy said that Nanny doesn't want to see me anymore." They were almost at Joyce's house by now.

"I'll tell you what I'll do. When we get to Nanny's you stay in the car while I have a talk to her. Then if she wants to see you I'll let you know. How does that sound?" suggested Mrs Albright, unsure whether or not she was doing the right thing.

"Okay" replied Mandy, "I hope she does want to see me. I've missed her a lot." They pulled up outside the house and Mandy stayed inside the car while her teacher walked up to the front door and rang the bell. She was nervous after the conversation she had just had with Mandy.

Chapter 8

"Mrs Croft?" asked Mrs Albright.

"Yes." replied Joyce with a puzzled expression on her face.

"I'm sorry to trouble you but I wasn't really sure what to do for the best. I'm from the primary school and I teach your Granddaughter, Mandy. The thing is, Mandy's mum didn't show up to pick her up from school this afternoon so I gave her a lift home, but there was no sign of her mum there either. I also had your address written down in case she wasn't there. Now the problem is that on the way here Mandy was worried that you might not want to see her."

"Did she say why I might not want to see her?"

"She did say something about you and her mother having some sort of argument, perhaps she just got her wires crossed. Is it okay to fetch her from the car then?"

"Yes of course, she's welcome here anytime." Joyce waited at the front door while the teacher went back to the car to get Mandy. She didn't have long to wait before the little girl was running up the path, arms held out to give her a big hug.

"Hello Darling, how are you? I haven't seen you for such a long time," said Joyce. "Why don't you go on in and find Granfy, he'll be surprised to see you." Mandy ran into the house, calling her Grandfather. Joyce turned to the teacher.

"Don't worry, she'll be fine here. I'll call her mum later to let her know where she is."

"Okay," replied Mrs Albright, "I've put a note through her door anyway, so when she gets back she'll know straightaway where Mandy is. Oh, by the way, when I tried to phone earlier there was no tone. Perhaps there's a fault on the line. Could you just let Mrs Croft know?"

"Yes of course. Thank you for bringing Mandy here. She'll see you at school tomorrow." The two ladies said their goodbyes and Joyce went back in the house. She went into the kitchen and made Mandy a glass of squash before returning to the lounge.

"So, how are you darling? How do you like school?"

"I love it, Nanny," replied Mandy excitedly, "we do lots of painting and drawing, and I've got lots of friends to play with."

"That's wonderful Mandy. And how is Mummy?" Joyce noticed the expression on Mandy's face change when her mum was mentioned.

"She's okay," she said, quietly. The excitement seemed to drain from her and she just sat without saying anymore.

"What is it darling?" asked Joyce.

"Oh, it's nothing, Nanny."

"Come on, you can tell me can't you?" Joyce put her arms around her granddaughter as the little girl burst into tears. "Mandy darling, if there's anything wrong you must tell us."

"It's just that Mummy is always shouting at me. I don't know what I keep doing wrong. She keeps telling me to get out of the house so I hide in the shed till its dark then I go to bed. She doesn't even say goodnight to me some nights."

"Does this happen all the time?" asked Joyce.

"No, sometimes she's nice to me. If she's awake when I get up it means she's in a good mood, but if she's asleep in the lounge it means she's going to wake up in a bad mood. That's when I have to stay out of her way." Joyce couldn't believe what she was hearing. She couldn't stop herself from asking the next question.

"Mandy darling, does Mummy ever hit you?"

Mandy bowed her head. She didn't want to get Mummy into trouble.

"Yes, but it's my fault because I get in her way," the little girl still had tears in her eyes, "You won't tell Mummy I told you, will you Nanny? She'll get very cross and hit me again. She said I'm not allowed to talk to you or Granfy."

"Don't worry Mandy, I won't tell Mummy." Joyce was struggling to stop herself from crying. She knew something wasn't right and hadn't done anything about it. Now she was more determined than ever. Nobody was going to harm her Granddaughter, she would make sure of it. She sat cuddling Mandy for a few minutes until she had stopped crying, and got up to make some dinner.

"Right, who's hungry?" she asked, trying to be cheerful.

"Me!" replied Viv, realising that his wife was trying to lighten up the atmosphere, "What about you, young lady?" he said looking at Mandy.

"Yeah, I'm starved!" she answered. "Can I help you make dinner, Nanny?"

"Of course you can. What shall we have?"

"Can we have chips please? I haven't had chips for ages. Mummy doesn't cook very much now."

"Chips it is!" said Joyce placing the chip pan on the stove to heat up. "Why doesn't Mummy cook very much now? Do you get takeaways then?"

"No, if Mummy's in a bad mood we don't have dinner."

"Are you telling me that some days you don't have anything to eat?"

"We'll I do because when I go out to the shed I've got a secret box that I keep biscuits and sweets in. Mummy never goes outside anymore so she doesn't know it's there." Mandy sounded much older than her five years; in a short space of time she had begun to learn how to fend for herself. Her childlike ways were disappearing much too soon. Joyce felt awful, knowing that sooner or later Ruby would be round to collect her daughter. She would have to be very careful what she said to her; if she found out that Mandy had said anything who knows what the consequences would be. Joyce decided that first thing the next morning she would telephone Social Services again, and tell them that this time maybe they should make an unplanned visit. That way Ruby wouldn't have a chance to hide any evidence of her drinking habit. The only problem

86

was that she would have to let Mandy go back home with her mother, something that she was very reluctant to do. Joyce took some potatoes from the plastic vegetable rack and took them over to the sink to peel. She spoke to Mandy who was by now sat at the kitchen table, watching her Grandmother.

"Listen Mandy, your Mummy will most probably be round soon to collect you. I don't want you to go but if we're to sort out the problem of her hitting you and shouting at you, you're going to have to go back with her tonight. That way she won't know anything about what we've talked about."

"But what if she asks what we've been saying?" Mandy asked, uncomfortable with the idea of lying to her mum.

"You can tell her that we talked about school and your new friends, or anything else you can think of, but whatever you do Darling you mustn't tell her that I know about her hitting you."

"Don't worry Nanny, I won't say anything." Mandy watched as Joyce finished peeling the potatoes and put them into the hot fat in the chip pan, after which she lit the grill and placed some sausages under the flame. While the dinner was cooking Viv joined them in the kitchen and began telling jokes, so while eating their meal the three of them took it in turns to tell another silly joke. Mandy hadn't laughed so much for months, forgetting all about her problems and being a normal five year old again. Once dinner was finished Mandy joined her Grandparents in the lounge.

"The washing up can wait," said Joyce, knowing in the back of her mind that once Ruby came to collect Mandy it may be quite a while before they saw her again.

By now it was about 6.30p.m. Ruby opened her eyes slowly and looked around the room. She raised her head a few inches and then lay it back down as the throbbing started. 'It must be time to get Mandy soon,' she thought to herself as she forced herself up into a sitting position. She looked at the clock, but couldn't quite make out the numbers. She rubbed her eyes and looked again.

"Oh my God! Mandy!" Ruby stood up quickly, ignoring the pounding in her head and went over to the phone. She picked up the receiver to telephone the school only to hear the continuous tone.

"Shit!" She had realised that her phone had been cut off. She ran into the hallway to find her shoes that she had kicked off earlier that day, she would have to run round to the phone box. As Ruby went to open the front door she saw the note that had been posted through the letterbox. She picked it up and began to read.

Mrs Croft, I brought Mandy home from school earlier as no-one turned up to pick her up but there was nobody here so I have taken her to her Grandparent's house. I hope there is no problem and you are okay,

Mrs M Albright. (Teacher)'

"Great, that's all I need," muttered Ruby to herself. Still, at least Mandy was safe. She went back into the kitchen and lit a cigarette. If Mandy was at Joyce's then she could take her time. She put the kettle on to make a coffee, she knew she would have to sober up a bit before facing her in-laws. Once she had drunk her coffee Ruby went out and walked up to the phone box. She dialled the number and waited for the signal to put the coin in the slot.

"Hello, Joyce?"

"Ruby, I wondered when you were going to call. Where have you been?" asked Joyce, trying not to let the anger show in her voice.

"I'm sorry, I wasn't well and laid on the sofa for an hour before I had to pick Mandy up but I fell asleep. Is she alright?"

"Yes, she's fine. She's had her dinner and she's playing with Viv at the moment."

"I'll be over as quick as I can to fetch her, I'll have to get the bus though because the car's playing up." There was nothing wrong with the car but Ruby knew she had drunk far too much to be in any fit state to drive.

"Don't worry, I'll bring her home. We'll be about half an hour, see you then." Joyce was finding it so difficult to be pleasant but knew that she would have to be for Mandy's sake.

"Okay," replied Ruby and replaced the handset. She hurried back home and quickly tidied up, hiding any empty vodka bottles just in case Joyce came in when she got there.

At the other end of the line Joyce put back the phone and called Mandy.

"That was Mummy on the phone. I've told her that I'll drop you off, so come and get your school things ready."

"But I don't want to go, Nanny. Can I stay here with you and Granfy?"

"I really wish you could darling, but don't worry, we'll see you very soon. By the time you get back it'll be bedtime, so you can just say goodnight to Mummy and go up. That way you don't have to worry about saying anything you shouldn't."

"But what if she's in a bad mood?" Mandy was sounding really worried; she had been with Nanny after her Mummy had told her not to.

"I don't think she'll be in a mood Darling, she sounded fine on the phone just now. If you have any problems tonight or tomorrow morning tell your teacher at school. I'll be phoning the school in the morning so they know what's going on."

"Okay, Nanny." Mandy collected her things together and said goodbye to Granfy. She didn't speak on the way home and Joyce didn't try to make her. She felt terrible taking her back home but knew it was probably the only way to handle the situation. They pulled up outside the house and Joyce switched off the engine. They both got out of the car and walked hand in hand up the pathway to the front door. Before they had a chance to ring the bell Ruby opened the door.

"Hello sweetie. I'm sorry I didn't pick you up from school earlier but I wasn't feeling well and fell asleep. I was really worried when I woke up and saw that it was gone 6 o'clock," Ruby genuinely sounded sorry, which surprised Joyce.

"Thanks Joyce, I hope she wasn't too much trouble." The way Ruby spoke to Joyce was such a contrast from the last time the two women were face to face. There was no mention of the altercation that had taken place that same morning.

"No, she never is. She's very tired though so I think she may want an early night." Joyce turned to Mandy. "Where's my hug then?" The little girl put her arms out and gave her Nanny the tightest hug she could.

"Bye, Nanny."

"Bye, bye Darling. See you soon," said Joyce as she gave Mandy a wink, unnoticed by Ruby. Mandy knew what her Grandmother meant and took comfort in the fact that Nanny would help her. Joyce said goodbye to Ruby and left the two of them at the door. A wave of guilt swept over her as she got into her car and drove back home. She couldn't sleep that night, worrying about her Granddaughter and what she was going to do about it.

Back inside her own house Mandy headed for the stairs, but was stopped in her tracks.

"Are you not talking to me then sweetie?" asked Ruby.

"Sorry Mummy, I thought it was bed time," replied Mandy.

"Well yes I suppose it is. Why don't you come and have a drink first, then you can tell me what you did at Nanny's." The little girl turned and followed her mum into the kitchen. Ruby made some squash and put it on the table in front of her daughter.

"So, did you have a good time today?" Ruby sounded genuinely interested, there was no nastiness in her voice, which made Mandy a little more at ease.

"Yes, I played cards with Granfy. We played snap and I won!"

"Well done. How is Granfy?"

"Oh, he's alright. He said he was pleased to see me. He told us jokes when we were eating dinner. Do you want to hear one Mummy?"

"Go on then, just one." Ruby seemed to be making an effort this evening, she was feeling guilty about not picking Mandy up and was doing her best to make up for it even though she still had a terrible headache from the alcohol she had drunk earlier.

"What do you call a deer with no eyes?"

"I don't know."

"No-eye-deer!"

"That's very good sweetie," laughed Ruby. "You'll have to tell that one to your friends at school tomorrow. Come on then, let's get you up to bed, it's getting late." Mandy stood up and headed for the stairs. Ruby followed, tucking her into bed.

"I like it when you come up and say goodnight to me, Mummy."

"Yes I know sweetie, but sometimes I don't feel too well and fall asleep."

"Is it because of that funny water you drink Mummy?" Mandy was so innocent. She didn't know what alcohol was or what effects it had on people. All she knew was that every time her mum drunk it she fell asleep and woke up in a bad mood. Ruby's attitude suddenly changed.

"What's Nanny said to you? Has she told you that I drink too much?"

"No Mummy. Nanny hasn't said anything." Mandy started trembling. She realised that she had said the wrong thing.

"If you're lying to me and I find out you've been talking about me to Nanny or anyone else there'll be trouble, you hear?"

"Yes Mummy, but I didn't say anything, I promise." Mandy was terrified and just wanted Mummy to go and leave her on her own. That way she couldn't accidentally say something she shouldn't. She was relieved when Ruby gave her the benefit of the doubt and said goodnight. Mandy put her head under the covers and wriggled to get comfortable in the put- you- up bed. The metal springs creaking with every movement. She found it hard getting to sleep though, worried what Mummy would do when she found out that she had told Nanny.

Downstairs Ruby poured herself a vodka. She needed one after the efforts of being pleasant to Joyce. As she took the first sip all the feelings of guilt for having neglected her daughter earlier disappeared. By the time she had finished her third glass she almost forgotten she had a daughter asleep upstairs. Within a couple of hours the usual pattern of events unfolded, with Ruby on the sofa, not in a fit state to do anything but sleep.

Morning came all too soon for Mandy, who woke up to find herself on a wet bed, the thin foam mattress on the temporary bed soaked through to the bottom. It was the first time she had wet since that awful day when Mummy found out and made her have that scolding hot bath. There was no way that she could tell her mum now, so the little girl just made the bed as if nothing was amiss, got herself dressed and went downstairs for breakfast. Once down stairs she noticed the lounge door open and peeped inside. Ruby was asleep, the coffee table in front of her displaying the evidence of last night's binge, empty bottles and an ashtray filled to the brim with dog ends. Mandy crept into the kitchen to make her own breakfast. She looked in the cupboard but there were no cereals left. Mummy needed to do some food shopping again. She looked along the worktop and found some bread and an almost empty packet of butter, which had been left out of the fridge all night. Mandy found a knife and spread the butter on the slice of bread as best she could. That was her breakfast that morning. She thought it must be time for school but couldn't tell the time, she would have to wake Mummy up to take her. This the little girl was not looking forward to. Slowly Mandy went into the lounge and over to where her mum was sleeping. Very gently she nudged Ruby's arm. Nothing. She plucked up some more courage and nudged a little harder as she began to speak.

"Mummy, wake up." Mandy moved back slightly as her mum stirred.

"What," groaned Ruby as she turned slightly onto her back. She opened her eyes slowly and saw her daughter standing in front of her.

"Mummy I think it's time to go now," replied Mandy, afraid of the response she would get from her mother.

"Go away," was all that Ruby managed to utter from under the blanket, which partly covered her face.

"But I've got school today, Mummy." Mandy stepped back slightly as her mother struggled to raise her throbbing head.

"Well if it means that much to you then bloody walk yourself," Ruby growled. Mandy knew she shouldn't ask the next question but it just seemed to come out.

"What about my lunch?" Ruby sat up, suddenly forgetting about the hangover. Mandy almost ran out of the way as her mother stood and walked into the kitchen. Ruby looked in the bread bin, but Mandy had just used the last slice for her breakfast. She then looked in the fridge but after finding it empty slammed the door in temper.

"Well you'll just have to go without, won't you?" Ruby glared at her daughter with such an evil look that poor little Mandy didn't dare argue.

"Okay Mummy. Is it time to go now?"

"Yes, and get a move on, you're getting on my nerves."

"Am I really walking on my own, Mummy?" asked Mandy, worried about crossing the busy roads. After all, she still was only five years old.

"Is that a problem then? Do I have to do everything for you? Surely you're not so stupid that

you can't put one foot in front of another are you?"
Ruby was seething with rage as she spoke. Mandy
knew she had to get out of the house quickly before
the shouting turned into hitting.

"No Mummy," she answered as she walked
into the hallway and picked up her coat, which was
hung on the banister. As she reached the front door
she heard her mother's voice right behind her.

"And if I'm not there to pick you up after
school you just come straight home. Under no
circumstances are you to get a lift from your
teacher. Do you hear me?"

"Yes Mummy," replied Mandy as she
opened the door and walked out.

Mandy walked the way her and her mum
went every morning. Somehow it seemed different
walking on her own. The traffic in the road seemed
faster and louder, the street seemed longer. As she
walked a woman with a young toddler in a
pushchair came the other way. The toddler dropped
a toy and the woman laughed as she picked it up
and gave it back. The toddler pointed at Mandy as
their paths crossed. Mandy smiled back shyly and
quickened her pace. Soon she was at the zebra
crossing. She waited for the traffic to stop and then
crossed. Once across she could see the welcome
sight of the school entrance. Mandy noticed that
there were no children in the playground. The only
people around were one or two mothers having a
chat before going their separate ways to do their
housework or shopping. The little girl realised that
she was late and ran into school, hung her coat up
on her allocated peg and ran into the classroom. Mrs

Albright was in the middle of taking the register. She looked up as Mandy entered the room and sat down.

Chapter 9

"Good morning Mandy, you're just in time. I almost had you marked down as absent."

"I'm sorry, Mrs Albright, I didn't know what time it was."

"Don't worry, Mandy. We're all late sometime or other." This put Mandy at ease and she settled down to a pleasant morning at school. When the bell rang for first play the teacher called Mandy back. She waited until all the children had left and spoke softly to the little girl.

"Are you okay this morning Mandy?"

"Yes I'm fine."

"Did you get back home to Mummy last night?"

"Yes, thank you." Mandy's voice went very quiet, almost inaudible. Mrs Albright noticed the sudden change and became concerned.

"Mandy, if there's anything troubling you, you know you can talk to me or any of the teachers here, don't you?" Mandy just nodded. She wanted to tell her teacher so much but knew that if Mummy ever found out she would be in so much trouble.

"Go on out and find your friends then. We can't have you missing playtime, can we?" said Mrs Albright, watching as Mandy walked out of the classroom and into the playground to join her friends. Something wasn't right. Mandy was such a friendly, happy little girl, and this just wasn't like her at all. The teacher made her way to the school office. She felt she had to talk to Mrs Wade, the head about her concerns. As she reached the office Mrs Wade was coming the other way.

"Ah, Mrs Albright. Just the person I was looking for. Would you mind coming in to my office for a minute?"

"That's funny, I was just on my way to see you," said Mrs Albright as the two of them entered the head's office, "I'm rather worried about little Mandy Croft. She doesn't seem to be herself this morning. I've asked her if there is anything wrong but she seems reluctant to tell me anything."

"Well I've just had a telephone call from her Grandmother. She is extremely worried about Mandy's situation at home. It seems her mother may have an alcohol problem."

"Oh no," answered the younger teacher. "Have the Social Services been called?"

"Apparently the Grandmother notified them a few months ago and they made a home visit but couldn't see a problem so they closed the case," replied the Head teacher.

"Is there nothing we can do?" asked Mrs Albright.

"All we can do at the moment is keep an eye on Mandy. If we see any sign of things getting worse, or God forbid any sign of physical abuse then we can contact Social Services ourselves. Unfortunately until then there's not a great deal we can do."

"That poor girl," sighed the teacher. "She is such a sweetie. I'll keep a close eye on her, don't you worry."

"Thanks. I wish there was more we could do, but we can't interfere without substantial evidence to back us up." The two teachers stood up and Mrs Albright made her exit. As she returned to the classroom the children were just returning from their playtime. Mandy came in with two of her friends and looked at Mrs Albright. The teacher gave her a warm smile, which the little girl returned, shyly. The rest of the morning passed quickly, it always did when the children were allowed to paint. Soon the lunchtime bell rang and the children ran out to the hallway just outside the classroom where their lunchboxes were kept. Mandy remained in the classroom though, remembering that she had no lunch that day. Mrs Albright noticed her sitting on her own.

"Mandy, aren't you going to get your lunch?"

"I haven't got any lunch today," she wanted to tell her teacher the real reason why she had no lunch but knew that she couldn't. "I left it at home."

"Well we can't have you going without, can we? Has anybody got anything in their lunchbox that they could possibly share with Mandy?" she asked out loud. As she looked around the classroom there was no shortage of willingness to share. Mandy was so well liked by everybody that they all wanted to help. Mrs Albright picked a few bits from three or four lunchboxes and placed them on a paper towel in front of Mandy. Then she went back to her own desk where she reached inside her bag. She pulled out a small carton of fresh orange juice and returned to where Mandy was sat.

"I hope you like orange juice," she said as she detached the straw from the side of the carton. Mandy's face lit up. She loved it. It was a long time since Mummy had brought orange juice.

"Thank you," said the little girl to the teacher as she tucked into her lunch. She knew this was better than anything Mummy would make for dinner tonight if she was still in the mood she was in this morning. Lunchtime was soon over and the afternoon went far too quickly for Mandy. The nearer it got to the end of the day the quieter she became. Ten minutes before the end of the day Mrs Albright told the children to help tidy away the pencils and books they had used. As soon as she realised it was almost time for home Mandy felt a sickly feeling inside. She looked outside to the playground where all the mothers were gathering to pick up their children. As yet there was no sign of her own mum. The tidying was finished and the children all sat at their tables waiting for the bell. Mandy almost jumped when it did finally ring, and began shaking. She didn't know why but she was actually frightened to be going home that day.

Once out in the playground Mandy watched while all her friends one by one found their parents and walked out of the school grounds. She waited in the usual place for her own mother but there was no sign. Inside Mrs Albright could see the little girl waiting so she headed out to wait with her.

"Mummy not here again Mandy?" she asked as she reached where the five year old was standing. Mandy shook her head without saying anything.

Suddenly they both heard a shout from outside the school gates.

"Mandy, sweetheart!" Ruby was running through the gate, waving at her daughter. "I'm sorry, I didn't realise what time it was."

"That's ok Mummy," replied Mandy as she took her mum's hand. Ruby turned to Mrs Albright.

"Thanks for waiting with Mandy. I just can't seem to keep track of the time lately. Oh, and by the way, thanks for taking her to my mother-in-laws yesterday."

The teacher could smell the alcohol on Ruby's breath as she spoke.

"That's no problem Mrs Croft. I think Mandy quite enjoyed the car ride." She watched as mother and daughter walked out of the school grounds and down the road. She wondered what sort of evening that poor little girl would have tonight.

Once down the road Ruby let go of her daughter's hand.

"You don't need me to prop you up, you're quite capable of walking by yourself." She was obviously still in a bad mood from that same morning. As they reached the corner shop she stopped abruptly.

"Wait here a minute."

Mandy did as she was told and waited while her mother entered the shop. She watched in the window while Ruby went straight to the counter and bought two large bottles of vodka. She came out again, ignoring her daughter and started to walk quickly towards home. Mandy followed a few paces behind, struggling to keep up. Once back home Ruby found her front door key in her pocket. With the two bottles held tightly in one hand she attempted to put the key in the lock but lost her grip and it fell to the doorstep, bounced and then fell on the ground.

"Shit!" She looked around on the ground but could not see where the key had landed. She looked towards Mandy who had only just caught up.

"Get that key," she ordered. Mandy looked around but she too couldn't see where the key had landed.

"Hurry up will you, I haven't got all day," Ruby screeched. Mandy quickly went down on her knees to look closer. She found the key; it had fallen almost under a large stone at the edge of the step. She picked it up and handed it to her mother who snatched it out of her hand.

"A snail could have done it quicker," she muttered under her breath as they both entered the house. Ruby headed straight for the lounge and the mini-bar where she poured a drink from one of the bottles. Mandy went into the kitchen. She was hoping that Mummy had been shopping but her hopes were soon dashed when she saw that the kitchen was in the same state it had been when she had left for school that morning. She knew in the back of her mind that there would be no dinner tonight. As she walked back into the hallway Mandy glanced into the lounge. She could see her mother settling down on the sofa with a full glass in her hand. It was going to be another lonely night for the five year old, with very little chance of any dinner. Mandy knew it wouldn't be long before Mummy was asleep and decided to wait until then to come back down and search for something to eat. She went upstairs and played with her dolls for about half an hour before very quietly creeping back down the stairs.

As she passed the lounge door Mandy glanced in to check. Sure enough Mummy was sound asleep, so she crept into the kitchen. She pulled a chair across to the worktop and climbed up in order to see if there was anything she could eat. There was an opened bread bag at the back of the worktop surface so Mandy stretched on tiptoes to reach. The bag was just out of reach so she thought that maybe if she jumped high enough she could grab it. As she jumped though, the little girl's feet pushed the chair backwards and it tipped over. Mandy lost her grip and slipped back onto the floor, knocking her chin on the edge of the worktop as she did. As she hit the ground she fell backwards, hitting her head on the leg of the chair. Little Mandy put her hand up to her chin and burst into tears as she saw the blood on her fingers. Unsure what to do she just sat, sobbing.

From her semi-conscious state Ruby woke up, hearing the commotion in the kitchen. She sat up, swearing under her breath. On hearing her daughter crying she thought she had better get up and see what was going on.

"What the hell have you been doing?" asked Ruby, picking up the chair.

"I'm sorry Mummy. I was hungry, I wanted some dinner," sobbed Mandy. She put her hand up to her chin again. "Mummy look, I'm bleeding." Mandy really wanted her mum to hug her at this moment, but there was nothing. No sympathy or any sign of any emotion except anger.

"Get up and sort yourself out. I haven't got time for your stupidity," shouted Ruby, "and clear that mess up," she added, pointing to the blood that had dripped onto the floor. Ruby went out of the kitchen and came back a couple of minutes later with a lit cigarette and an ashtray in her hand. She sat at the kitchen table and watched her daughter get a cloth from the draining board and wipe away the bloodstains on the floor. Mandy couldn't believe what she was being made to do. Not long ago if she hurt herself Mummy would give her a cuddle and make her a mug of warm milk to make her feel better. It seemed these days were over; Mummy had changed and each day seemed to be a little worse than the day before. Mandy finished what she was doing and looked at her mum.

"What are you staring at?" asked Ruby nastily.

"I was just going to ask if I could have some dinner," replied Mandy, realising at once that she shouldn't have asked. Ruby grabbed her arm tightly and pulled it towards her, forcing the little girl's hand onto the table. The tears started streaming down Mandy's face. She was terrified of what might happen next. Still holding her daughter's arm in one hand Ruby took a long drag of her cigarette and exhaled the smoke straight into Mandy's face. The little girl turned her head away to escape the smoke, which was stinging her eyes. Ruby suddenly yanked Mandy's tiny arm, jolting the little girl towards her.

"Look at me, I haven't finished with you yet."

Mandy looked straight at her mother, who took another drag of her cigarette before speaking again.

"Did you have lunch at school today?"

"Yes."

"Then you don't need feeding now, do you?"

"But I'm hungry, Mummy," cried Mandy, the tears still running down her face.

"Well that's just tough, isn't it?"

Mandy cried louder, this just wasn't happening to her. At this moment all she wanted was Nanny. She would help her. As the crying got louder Ruby became angrier.

"If you don't shut that noise I'll give you something to cry for," she threatened, but Mandy just couldn't stop herself. Then as if the situation could get any worse the little girl wet herself. She just stood as she felt the wet pour down her leg and splash onto the floor. Ruby almost screeched at the little girl as she saw what was happening.

"You dirty little animal!" Ruby's eyes had turned evil as she looked at her daughter, and still holding the half-smoked cigarette she stabbed it onto the back of the little girl's tiny hand. Mandy screamed as her mother held the burning end and twisted it, searing through the delicate skin. She tried to pull her hand away but the more she struggled the harder her mother pressed. As she pulled the cigarette away Ruby released the grip from Mandy's arm.

"That's how animals get treated, now get out of my sight."

Mandy ran from the kitchen, almost tripping over in her rush to get away from this mad woman. She ran up the stairs and into the bathroom where she turned on the cold tap and put her hand under the running water, the pain almost unbearable. Through the water she could see the dark red mark that was left on her hand. The little girl stood for about five minutes with her hand under the water, afraid to take it out and see the extent of the damage her mother had caused. As she stood, Mandy looked up into the bathroom mirror. Looking back at her was a tiny pale face, eyes red from the tears. All around her mouth were bloodstains mixed with the tearstains. The little girl found a flannel and wiped away the stains, revealing a deep cut along the bottom of her chin. As she looked at her own reflection wiping her face she noticed the scar on her hand. The skin had been literally burned away, leaving a cigarette-sized circle of raw flesh underneath. Mandy felt sick. She just couldn't comprehend what had happened to her, and all because she wanted something to eat.

After cleaning herself up as best she could Mandy took off her wet underwear and clothes and took herself into her room. She put on her nightdress and got into bed. The little girl was exhausted and frightened. She spoke quietly to herself as she rocked herself to sleep, holding her painful hand in the other: 'Daddy if you can see me from Heaven, please help me.'

Chapter 10

Downstairs Ruby put what was left of her cigarette in the ashtray. She got up and headed for the lounge to pour yet another vodka. She sat down with her drink. There was no remorse for the evil she had just committed; it was as if it had never happened. Within an hour or so Ruby had drunk herself unconscious again. At least in this state no harm would come to little Mandy asleep upstairs.

The pain in Mandy's hand and chin caused her to wake up early the following morning. She got out of bed, realising that she had wet again and walked over to the bedroom door where she put her ear against it. There was no sound from downstairs, which meant that Mummy must still be asleep. That was a good sign. If she was quiet enough Mandy had planned to get dressed and creep out of the house as quickly as possible. She moved to where she had put her school uniform the night before and started to put on her blouse. As she put it on she noticed the smudged bloodstains on the front of it. Mandy knew there were no clean blouses in the cupboard for her to wear; Mummy hadn't done any washing for a long time. She just hoped that her jumper would cover the worst of it, which fortunately it did. She opened the underwear draw to find a clean pair of knickers and some socks but the draw was empty. Mandy knew she couldn't wear yesterday's as they were wet, so she looked around the room where she found a pair of socks that hadn't yet been put in the washing basket and put them on. She couldn't find any knickers though, so she just put on her skirt and headed downstairs as quietly as possible.

From the bottom of the stairs Mandy could just see into the lounge where her mother was still barely conscious. She put on her shoes, which were by the front door and took her coat from the banister. Very carefully she pulled down the catch on the door and opened it towards her. When the gap was big enough for her to get through Mandy crept out, closing it as quietly as she could behind her. She breathed a sigh of relief before running fifty yards or so up the street. Only then did Mandy stop to put on her coat and catch her breath. As she walked on Mandy inspected the injury on her hand. It was still extremely painful to touch. She knew that she would have to hide her hand from her teacher; if Mummy found out she had told anyone she would be in deep trouble. Mandy trembled inside at the thought of Mummy punishing her again.

Soon enough the school entrance was in sight but there was no one around except for the caretaker who was just unlocking the gate.

"You're early, young lady," said Mr Smithson, noticing the young pupil.

"Am I?"

"Yes, it's only 8.30. Is your Mummy not with you?

"She's, um, still in bed. She's not very well," replied Mandy, trying to sound as grown up as possible.

"Oh dear, I hope it's nothing serious. Do you want to wait inside, it's a bit chilly out here this morning?"

"No thanks, I'll wait outside." She did really want to go in the warm but was worried about her teacher asking questions when she noticed her sitting on her own.

"Okay, I'm sure your friends will be here soon." The caretaker opened the gate wide and headed back indoors. Mandy walked across the empty playground to a bench situated in front of one of the classrooms. It wasn't long before the playground started filling up with children, including a few of the little girl's friends.

"Hi, Mandy," came a happy voice running towards her, "what happened to your chin?"

"Hi Rachel, I fell off a chair," answered Mandy, suddenly conscious of her injuries from the night before. She put up her hand to try and hide the cut on her chin but in doing so she revealed the horrific burn mark on her hand.

"What's that on your hand?" asked Rachel, quick to notice the scar.

"Nothing."

Mandy quickly put her arm down, pulling the sleeve of her coat over her hand. Another friend ran towards the two of them, distracting Rachel from asking any more questions.

"What have you done to your chin?" asked Shelley.

"Nothing," replied Mandy, putting her head down to try and hide her face.

"She fell off a chair," interrupted Rachel, "and she's got a mark on her hand."

"Let me see," asked Shelley, pulling at Mandy's arm.

"Get off me," shouted Mandy as she pulled her arm away from her friend and ran away. She ran round the side of the building where she was out of view of the playground. The two girls left behind just looked at each other, not sure what they had done to upset their friend.

Mandy sat down with her back against the building wall and her legs stretched out in front of her. She began to cry. Now her friends had seen the mark on her hand they would surely tell the teacher, who in turn would say something to Mummy. And when Mummy found out she would be really cross and do something horrible as punishment.

The two friends decided to try and comfort Mandy, so they followed her to the side of the building. One of them put their arm around her while the other spoke.

"What's wrong Mandy? We weren't being horrible, we just wanted to know how you hurt yourself."

"I told you, I fell off a chair."

"But what about your hand?" asked Rachel.

"I knocked it when I fell," answered Mandy looking up at her two friends, "please don't tell anyone."

"Okay we won't," they both replied together. At five years old they didn't think there could be any other possible cause for Mandy's injuries, and as she was their friend they respected her wishes and promised not to say anything, not knowing that the best thing they could do was tell their teacher. The two girls managed to cheer Mandy up slightly and when the bell rang they walked into class together.

"Good morning children," Mrs Albright greeted the class.

"Good-morning-Mrs Albright," came the reply in harmony from the twenty-five pupils. The class settled into the first part of the day happily. Mandy somehow managed to keep her hand covered using the sleeve of her jumper. It was still painful and the slightly coarse wool fabric from the cuff seemed to aggravate it even more, but she kept it covered, there was no way that she was going to let anyone else see it. Mrs Albright kept an eye on Mandy during the morning. She had spotted the cut on her chin and asked about it but Mandy stuck to her story, which technically was true. She did fall off a chair. What Mandy omitted to tell her teacher was the reason she fell off a chair; the fact that she had only climbed on the chair because she was hungry and her mother was too drunk to bother making her something to eat.

The lunchtime bell rang and once again little Mandy sat still at her table while the rest of the class ran out to fetch their lunchboxes.

"No lunch again Mandy?" asked Mrs Albright.

"I'm sorry, I forgot to make it this morning," replied Mandy, looking worried, as if expecting to get told off. Mrs Albright frowned. Had she heard right, a five year old forgot to make her own lunch?

Why on earth would a five year old *need* to make her own lunch? She decided not to question Mandy about it anymore – the poor little girl looked frightened enough as it was.

Mrs Albright once again asked for donations from Mandy's classmates. The response was the same as the previous day and Mandy ended up with more food than she could manage to eat. Instead of throwing what was left away though, Mandy thought ahead. She knew the chances of getting anything to eat later were pretty slim, so she wrapped up the sandwich and chocolate bar that were left in a paper towel and slipped them into her coat pocket. Mrs Albright saw what the little girl did but said nothing.

Once all the children had finished their lunch they went outside to play for the half-hour or so until time for the afternoon bell. The teacher stayed inside and watched the children out of the window. She noticed that Mandy wasn't playing. Instead she sat on the bench watching her friends. Mrs Albright watched Mandy's two best friends walk up to her but was surprised to see them walk away again a few moments later, leaving the little girl on her own. She decided to go out and see what the problem was. Within a couple of minutes the teacher was out in the playground. She caught the eye of Rachel and Shelley and beckoned them over.

"Yes Miss?" asked Rachel politely.

"Is there anything wrong with Mandy, you usually play with her don't you?

"She said she doesn't want to play today."

"Did she say anything else?" asked the teacher. The two girls looked at each other. They both knew that they should say something about the mark on Mandy's hand, but neither of them wanted to betray their friend. Mrs Albright sensed they were hiding something.

"Listen girls, if Mandy's got a problem then we need to help her sort it out."

"But we promised we wouldn't say anything," answered Shelley, "she's our friend and if we break our promise then we won't be friends anymore."

Mrs Albright knelt down to the girls' level and spoke softly to them both.

"I know she's your friend and you don't want to upset her, but if she's not very happy then we need to do what we can to make her happy again. The thing is, I can't begin to make her happy again if I don't know what the problem is. Do you understand my problem girls?" The teacher looked at the girls who both nodded. Rachel began to speak.

"I don't really know why Mandy's not happy. Maybe it's because she fell off a chair last night," suggested Shelley.

"Oh, you mean the cut on her chin?" asked Mrs Albright.

"Yes, but she's got a mark on her hand and when I asked her about it she started crying and ran away. Please don't tell her I told you, she won't be our friend anymore."

Mrs Albright thought for a moment. She hadn't noticed the mark on Mandy's hand. She told the two girls they had done the right thing by telling her and promised she wouldn't tell Mandy. The two girls walked away and carried on playing. Mrs Albright looked around the playground until she caught sight of Mandy sat on her own on the bench. She walked over and sat down next to the little girl.

"Hello Mandy."

"Hello," Mandy replied without looking up.

"You're very quiet today, is everything okay?"

"Yes thank you Miss."

"Is that cut on your chin hurting you?" asked the teacher.

"No not really." Mandy's instinct was to put her hand up to cover her chin but she couldn't let the teacher see that mark.

"If you like we could go into the medical room and put some cream on it to stop it getting infected."

"Okay," answered Mandy reluctantly. Mrs Albright held out her hand for the little girl to hold but Mandy pretended not to notice and kept her arms down by her side. The teacher realised what Mandy was doing and knew she had to somehow find a way to have a look at that hand. She put her arm on Mandy's shoulder as they both walked into the building and along the corridor to the medical room. The room was small with a desk along the left hand wall. At the far end of the room was a put-you-up bed, which children could lie down on if they felt ill. There was also a comfortable chair in the corner of the room. Mrs Albright invited Mandy to sit in the chair while she looked in the large first aid cupboard for some antiseptic cream.

"Here we are then," she said as she picked up the tube of cream, "now let's have a look at that chin." Mandy put her head back as her teacher first wiped over the cut with a wet tissue then carefully squeezed some of the antiseptic ointment onto her fingertip and rubbed it over the cut.

"That's rather a nasty cut you have there, Mandy. How did you say you did it?"

"I fell off a chair," Mandy quickly replied.

"And what on earth were you doing climbing on a chair?" asked the teacher softly.

"I, I...I was hungry and tried to reach some bread but my chair slipped and I fell back." Mandy suddenly burst into tears and sobbed uncontrollably. The teacher put her arms around the little girl and hugged her tightly.

"It's okay Darling," she whispered as the poor little girl cried and cried, unable to stop the tears. It was a good five minutes before Mandy began to calm down, the teacher still holding on to her tightly. After a few more minutes Mrs Albright released her grip and stood up to find some tissues.

"Here, wipe those eyes Darling." Mandy took the tissues and did as she was asked, letting out a sniffle every now and then. She looked at her teacher, her eyes red from all the tears.

"I'm sorry for crying," the little girl apologised.

"There's nothing to be sorry for Mandy; we all need to have a good cry every now and again."

"You won't tell my Mummy, will you?" Mandy asked, suddenly looking afraid.

"No, not if you don't want me to," replied the teacher, "but if there's a problem then your mum really should know."

"No, please," Mandy begged, "She'll be cross and hurt me ag…" Mandy stopped abruptly. She suddenly realised she had said too much. The teacher picked up on what had just happened and knelt down in front of Mandy.

"Listen carefully, if Mummy or anyone else is hurting you then you must tell me. You must understand that it's wrong for any child to be treated badly."

"But it's my fault. She needs to sleep all day and I keep waking her up."

"Why does she need to sleep all day, Mandy? Is she ill?"

"I don't know. All I know is that she drinks that funny water and it makes her in a bad mood and that's when I have to stay out of the way. If I stay out of the way then she can go to sleep on the sofa." The teacher was finding it difficult to hold back the tears.

"Mandy Darling, when you say 'hurt' you again, what do you mean?" Mandy didn't want to say anymore, she was already in enough trouble if Mummy found out what she had said.

"It doesn't really matter, I know she doesn't mean to do it. Please don't tell her what I said" The teacher sighed. She had to find out what else had been going on; the more she knew the better the chances of something being done about it.

"What about that mark on your hand, Mandy?" she asked seriously. The little girl quickly pulled her sleeve right the way over her hand.

"Please Mandy, let me see." Slowly Mandy pulled back her sleeve, revealing the horrific burn mark. Mrs Albright almost swore to herself as she looked at the raw circle where the skin had been scorched away. She knew straight away that it was a cigarette burn and couldn't possibly have been done accidentally.

"Mandy, please tell me why your mum did this to you."

"It was my fault, I looked away when she was talking to me and then I wet myself." Mrs Albright couldn't believe what she was hearing.

"So you mean she did this awful thing to you just because you had a little 'accident?'" The little girl nodded, close to tears once again. The teacher could see she was becoming distraught again and so refrained from asking any more questions. She helped Mandy to wipe her eyes and told her not to worry, as everything would be all right. She also put some antiseptic cream onto the cigarette burn and placed a square piece of lint over it, held in place by two small strips of transparent medical tape.

"There, that should keep it clean for now. Try not to get it too wet or it will take longer to get better," instructed the teacher. "Now, are you ready to go back to class? The bell will be ringing any minute now for afternoon lessons." Mandy nodded and stood up ready to go back to class. As she did so she looked up at her teacher, her face pale apart from the red around her eyes.

"You won't tell Mummy will you?"

"Don't you worry about that, Darling. I won't say a word to Mummy but I promise you I will do something about her hurting you. You just leave things to me and I'll do what I need to do." The little girl seemed reassured and went back to class where she joined her two best friends. Mrs Albright meanwhile, herself close to tears headed straight for the head teacher's office. She knocked on the door and waited for her signal to enter. Mrs Wade was sat behind her desk finishing her lunch. She sat down on the chair opposite the head as she began to speak.

"I've just been with little Mandy Croft again."

"Is it her mum's drinking?"

"Yes in a way, but it's far worse than we first thought."

"How do you mean?" asked the head, placing down her cup of tea.

"She's been…how can I put this…there's a cigarette burn on her hand."

"Are you sure?" Mrs Wade felt a sickly feeling inside as the other teacher explained what Mandy had told her less than ten minutes before.

"Yes I'm sure, but that's not all. It seems she drinks all the time and when she's not asleep on the sofa she's taking out her frustrations on poor little Mandy. That girl is terrified that I might say something to her mother, because she fears that if her mother knows she's been talking about her then she'll be punished again."

Mrs Wade sat back in her seat and sighed deeply.

"Right, we need to act. This just can't go on any longer. I'll telephone her grandmother and let her know what's happening, and then I'll phone the Social Services. Don't worry; I'll get this sorted straight away. Keep your eye on Mandy and I'll come and find you and her when I know what's going to happen. One thing's for sure, it can't go on."

"I agree," replied the younger teacher as the two women parted. Back in class, Mrs Albright kept the children busy first with a story and then spelling practice. She kept a close eye on Mandy, who seemed quieter than usual. Although she had the reassurance of her teacher she was worried about the consequences of her telling what had been happening at home.

In her office meanwhile, Mrs Wade dialled the telephone and waited for the reply.

"Hello", said the cheerful voice on the other end.

"Mrs Joyce Croft?" asked the head teacher. Joyce at once knew that something serious had happened. She listened carefully as Mrs Wade explained about the cut on Mandy's chin and the cigarette burn on her hand. A wave of guilt overcame her. She should have done something before the situation came to this.

"Have you contacted Social Services?" she asked.

"I'm about to do that now," answered the head, "I wanted to let you know what was happening before I did so."

"Thanks. I have telephoned them since the last time they visited but they insisted that unless there was any proof of any mistreatment of Mandy then the case would remain closed. I tried to argue with them but they said that the visiting officer was quite satisfied that there wasn't a problem."

"Well I think we have enough proof now, Mrs Croft. I'll phone them straightaway. We can't let this go."

"I agree totally. Please let me know what happens."

"Of course. I'll ring back straightaway. Goodbye Mrs Croft."

As Joyce slowly replaced the receiver she sat down; a feeling of helplessness to do anything overcame her. All she could do was pray that the Social Services would listen to Mrs Wade and do something.

Chapter 11

Mrs Wade took a deep breath before dialling the number for Social Services. As a head teacher she had the direct number to one of the more senior members. It wasn't long before Mr Lawrence answered the phone. He listened while Mrs Wade explained the situation and voiced her concerns about Mandy's welfare. Mr Lawrence found the file containing the report from the last home visit. He quickly read through it before speaking.

"I see from the paperwork in front of me that Mandy's mother may have a drinking problem, although the visiting officer, Mrs...er...oh yes, Mrs Howard, could not see any evidence of this."

"Perhaps Mrs Croft hid the evidence. It wouldn't be difficult, would it? From what my colleague has told me Mrs Croft spends a vast amount of time asleep on the sofa. She has spoken at quite some length to Mandy who tells her that her mother sleeps after drinking 'funny water'; now that in my experience is not something that a five year old would make up."

"Yes I do tend to agree. And you say she has a cigarette burn? Are you sure?"
Mrs Wade was becoming agitated. This poor little girl was suffering and it seemed so difficult to get something done about it. She raised her voice slightly as she spoke.

"Please don't take offence Mr Lawrence but I have been a head teacher for some years now and I know when a child is suffering. I have only once before seen a cigarette burn but it not something

123

that you forget. Now could you please send somebody round to visit Mrs Croft at her home and look at the poor girl's injuries?" The Social Worker was taken aback slightly by the tone in Mrs Wade's voice.

"Okay, I'll organise a home visit." He looked at the clock on the wall before continuing. "It's Friday afternoon and all the visiting officers are out on calls at the moment. I'll put this case on the priority list but I can't promise anything will be done today."

"Surely you must have an emergency procedure. Something needs to be done and quickly, before that poor girl is harmed anymore."

"Mrs Wade, I assure you that everything that can be done will be done, and if not today then definitely tomorrow." The head teacher sighed. She knew she wasn't going to get any further in the matter.

"So I have to send that girl back home for the weekend knowing that her mother could hurt her again?"

"I'm sorry Mrs Wade. We have such a backlog of calls to make and we are getting through them as quickly as possible. There is nothing more I can do. I will telephone you first thing on Monday morning and let you know the outcome."

"Alright, but please note that I'm not happy about sending Mandy back home to her mother." Mrs Wade said goodbye and replaced the receiver before banging her fist on the desk with frustration. She sat for a few moments before phoning Joyce back to explain what was going to happen.

"Thanks for trying, Mrs Wade," said Joyce after hearing about the conversation with Mr Lawrence. She was equally as frustrated as the head teacher, but knew there wasn't a lot more that could be done at that moment. She wanted to collect Mandy from school and take her back to her own house where she would be safe, but she knew that it would only make matters worse. All she could do was wait and pray that the Social Services would realise what was going on.

Back in the classroom it was getting near to home time. The children began packing away their pens and exercise books. Mandy once again began trembling at the thought of going home. The bell rang and the children waited for Mrs Albright to let them go. Before doing so she asked Mandy to wait behind for a few minutes. As the classroom emptied Mrs Wade came through the door. She pulled two small chairs over to Mrs Albright's desk and invited Mandy to sit down on one while she sat on the other. She put her hand on the young girl's knee.

"Mandy I've had a chat with someone from the Social Services. We are all very concerned about you. I've also spoken to your Nanny who is also very worried."

"Can I go and stay with Nanny?" asked Mandy excitedly.

"Unfortunately you can't at the moment. She would love to have you but you must go home with Mummy. I know you're worried about that but somebody is going to visit your Mummy and you tomorrow to see exactly what has been happening."

"Does Mummy know I told you about my hand?" asked Mandy, shaking with fear now as she considered the consequences.

"No, she doesn't know anything at the moment. That's why you must go home to her. That way she won't know anything about what you've told us." Mandy nodded and slowly got up to leave. Both teachers looked at each other and without speaking, both felt the same anxieties about letting the young girl go home for the weekend. As Mandy put on her coat Mrs Albright stood up.

"Would you like me to walk with you over to your Mummy?"

"No, I'm okay, thank you," replied Mandy. She wanted her teacher to stay with her but knew that if Mummy wasn't waiting for her she would have to sneak out of the school gate without anyone realising she was on her own. The teacher crouched down to Mandy's level and held her by both arms.

"Listen Mandy, try not to worry. Things will be sorted out, I promise. But when the Social Worker visits you must tell him or her what has been happening otherwise they can't do anything about it. I know it's difficult but you must be brave. Your mum needs help and this is the only way you and her will get the help you both need."

"I will tell them, I promise," said Mandy.

"Off you go then, have a good weekend," replied Mrs Albright as she stood up. Mandy said goodbye and hurried out of the classroom and into the playground. She looked around but there was no sign of Mummy. The little girl looked behind her to see if anyone was looking before running out of the school gate. Once down the road a bit Mandy slowed her pace. There was nothing at home to give her reason to hurry.

Once home Mandy rang the doorbell but there was no answer. This wasn't a good sign; it meant that Mummy was probably asleep on the sofa so inevitably she would wake up in a bad mood. The little girl walked around the side of the house to the back door, which was open. She crept into the kitchen, careful not to make a noise and wake her Mummy up. The kitchen was in the usual state, with empty vodka bottles scattered around along with overflowing ashtrays. The bin hadn't been emptied for days, with rubbish spilled out onto the floor. Mandy looked around to see if she could see any squash for her to drink but all she could find was an empty bottle so she pulled a chair up to the sink, rinsed out a dirty glass and poured herself some water. As she finished her drink Mandy heard her mum's voice from the lounge. She didn't sound very happy.

"Is that you Mandy?"

"Yes Mummy."

"Get your arse in here young lady," Ruby ordered. Mandy quickly took off her coat and went into the lounge.

"What time do you call this?" growled Ruby.

"I…I don't know, I can't tell the time."

"Don't be clever with me, you're late. Where have you been?"

"Nowhere, Mummy. I came straight home."

"You lying bitch. You've been messing about with your friends instead of coming straight home, haven't you?"

"No Mummy, I promise." Mandy knew it was going to be a bad night. She would be better staying out of her mum's way. She took a step towards the door when her mum suddenly grabbed her arm.

"Don't walk away from me when I'm talking to you. Who do you think you are?"

"I'm sorry, Mummy."

"I should think so too. Go and get my fags out of the kitchen, and hurry up." Mandy hurried into the kitchen, shaking with fear. She looked around but could not see any cigarettes. She started to cry because she knew she would be punished for not finding them. She jumped as her mother shouted from the lounge.

"For God's sake. How long does it take?"

"I can't find them, Mummy," Mandy replied. Ruby suddenly got up from her lying position and stormed into the kitchen. She yanked Mandy's arm so hard it almost dislocated from her shoulder.

"Get out of my way. I ask you to do one simple thing and you can't even do that properly, can you?" Mandy ran out of the kitchen before her mum had a chance to do anything else to her. As she climbed the stairs she could hear her mum swearing and throwing bottles and crockery around. Ruby herself could not find any cigarettes and so she took a long dog-end from one of the ashtrays. She lit what was left of the cigarette and sat down at the table. After one or two puffs she calmed down slightly. She called up to Mandy who had taken comfort in her dolls. The little came down the stairs and walked silently into the kitchen.

"I've got a headache, you'll have to get your own dinner tonight."

"Yes Mummy," Mandy didn't dare argue, "What shall I make?"

"I don't know, why don't you do yourself some beans on toast?" Ruby suggested, oblivious to the fact that she was asking her five-year-old daughter to do something completely absurd.

"I can't make beans on toast Mummy," Mandy replied, already trembling in anticipation of what was to come.

Ruby stormed over to the cupboard, took out the last tin of baked beans and slammed the door shut. She opened the tin, emptied the contents into a saucepan and put it on the stove to heat up. The first match snapped as Ruby struck the side of the matchbox, adding to her rage. The second match lit so Ruby ignited the gas ring. While the beans were heating up Ruby looked around for some bread but all that was left in the packet was a mouldy crust.

"You'll just have to have beans on their own," said Ruby matter-of-factly.

"Okay Mummy." Mandy knew better than to argue. She made her way to the table and pulled out a chair just far enough for her to climb on. Ruby stood in silence with her back to Mandy, watching the beans bubbling in the pan. She seemed to be in a trance, not noticing that the beans at the bottom of the pan were burning. Suddenly Ruby regained her concentration and turned off the heat. She looked in the cupboard for a clean bowl but there were none left, so she picked up the first one she could find, which had been used for cereal a couple of days previously. She rinsed it quickly under the tap, not bothering to wash off the stubborn remains of dried-on cereal, and placed it on the table in front of Mandy. She then picked up the pan and poured the scolding hot beans into the bowl.

Mandy realised she didn't have a spoon so she started to climb off the chair to fetch one.

"Where do you think you're going now?"

"I...I'm just getting a spoon Mummy."

"So why didn't you ask for one then?" shouted Ruby, reaching over to the draining board and picking up a spoon, not bothering to check whether or not it was clean. She slammed the spoon down on the table in front of Mandy, making the little girl jump. Mandy picked up the spoon but it slipped out of her trembling hand and fell to the floor.

"You clumsy little bitch, can't you do anything properly?"

"I'm sorry Mummy, it slipped out of my hand."

"*I'm sorry Mummy,*" repeated Ruby, nastily mimicking Mandy's little voice. "Well if you don't want to use a spoon then you'll have to eat like an animal, won't you?"

Ruby suddenly pushed Mandy's head from behind straight into the bowl of beans. Mandy tried to resist but her mother's strength and temper were no match for the little girl, the heat from the beans burning her delicate face. Ruby released her grip and Mandy lifted her head, tears streaming down her face by now.

"You can stop that stupid noise now or I'll really give you something to cry for."
Mandy held her breathe as she tried her best to stop the tears. Ruby picked up the spoon and slammed it back onto the table.

"Now get it eaten and get to bed. I don't want to see your ugly face again."
Ruby stormed out of the kitchen and back into the lounge, slamming the door behind her. Mandy sat still for a couple of minutes in total bewilderment, her face still stinging from the burning beans. She put her hand up to her face to wipe off the sauce that remained, the orange colour staining the square gauze patch that covered her cigarette burn. As Mandy looked at the patch she suddenly had an awful thought: What if Mummy had seen it? She would know that her teacher had seen the cigarette burn, which meant that Mandy had been talking about her. The little girl quickly tore off the patch and put it in the bin, but on returning to the table the kitchen door opened and Ruby walked in, glaring at her daughter.

"What are you doing now, you're supposed to be eating your dinner?" she screamed.

"Nothing Mummy."

"Don't lie to me you lying little bitch, you've just put something in the bin. Are you going to tell me what it is or do I have to look for myself?"

"It was nothing Mummy." Mandy was terrified by now for she knew that whatever she said or did next would have horrible consequences.

"So, we've got to do this the hard way, have we?" said Ruby as she grabbed her daughter's wrist tightly and dragged her over to the bin.

"Mummy you're hurting me," cried Mandy as the pain on the back of her hand became unbearable where her mother was squeezing so tightly.

"Well if you had answered me properly in the first place there wouldn't have been a problem, would there? Now show me what you've just put in the bin."

Mandy knew she would have to show her mother. Sooner or later she would find out so why not get it over with now? With her free hand Mandy reached to the bin and picked up the gauze patch, one side of it stained orange from the bean juice, and the other side yellow from where the burn had oozed. She opened her hand up and showed her mother.

"What on earth is that?" asked Ruby with a disgusted look on her face.

"It's a plaster for my hand."

"I can see that you stupid cow, what I want to know is who gave it to you?"

"My teacher," replied Mandy quietly, looking at the floor and somehow wishing that she could disappear under it.

Ruby almost exploded with rage as she suddenly pushed her daughter away from her with such a force that the little girl fell backwards.

"What have I told you about talking to people, especially do-gooders like your teacher? Do you want Social Services to come and take you away?"

Mandy managed to pick herself up from the floor and stood in front of her mother, shaking with fear. She really wanted to answer yes to that last question but knew the only answer she could give was no. She shook her head, still looking at the floor. Without warning Ruby grabbed the little girl's hair and pulled it back, forcing her daughter to look at her.

"I asked you a question. Do you want to be taken away and put in some home with other horrible children who don't know how to behave?"

Mandy's mouth opened and before she knew what she was saying the words came out.

"I want to be with Daddy. I don't want you; you're horrible. I want to be in Heaven with Daddy." Almost as soon as the words came out Mandy realised that she was really in for it this time. She tried to pull away but her mother was too quick for her.

"What did you say?" roared Ruby as she dragged Mandy by her hair over to the sink. With her free hand she picked up the washing up liquid bottle and squeezed, forcing the green liquid into the child's mouth.

"Please Mummy, no," cried Mandy as she fought to stop the liquid entering her mouth. She gagged as the foul-tasting liquid was forced down her throat. Ruby then pulled out the bottle and threw it into the sink, at the same time releasing her grip from Mandy's hair.

Mandy wiped her mouth with the back of her hands, still gagging as her mother began to shout again.

"Don't you ever talk to me like that again or this is what will happen. Who the hell do you think you are? You're a little bitch and I wish you were with your precious Daddy too. That way I wouldn't have to put up with you."

Mandy couldn't believe what she was hearing. Did Mummy really want her to be in Heaven with Daddy? By now the little girl was petrified. Her mother had turned into some kind of monster, like some horrible nightmare. She started to walk away but was grabbed by the arm and yanked around to face her mother.

"I haven't finished with you yet. I want to know what you've been saying to your teacher."

"N…nothing Mummy."

"I don't believe you. What did you tell her about your hand?"

"I said that I fell over."

"I hope for you sake that you're telling the truth. If I ever find out you're not I'll knock that lying mouth right off your shoulders. Do you understand?"

"Yes Mummy," answered Mandy, now even more terrified because she knew that Social Services were coming soon. If they didn't take her away Mummy would be crosser than she'd ever been before and would really hurt her. "Can I go now Mummy?"

"Yes, just get out of my sight. It's you who's driving me to drink. I don't want to see you again tonight, you hear me?" Ruby stormed out of the kitchen and into the lounge where she headed for the last remaining vodka bottle.

Mandy made sure her mother was settled in the lounge before getting herself a drink of water to wash away the taste of the washing-up liquid. Once she had done so as best she could the little girl crept quietly to her bedroom. She lay on her bed clutching a teddy close to her chest. She closed her eyes and began to think about what her teacher had told her earlier that day. Somebody would be round to see her and Mummy but she would have to tell them everything or they wouldn't be able to help her. After everything her mother had put her through, Mandy didn't want her to get into trouble. She also knew that it was wrong to tell lies, so what could she do?

Suddenly she sat up. There was only one way out of this predicament; she would run away. That way she wouldn't have to get Mummy into trouble but she wouldn't have to put up with Mummy's temper either. The little girl opened her wardrobe and took out the backpack that she used for school, taking out the pencil case and books that were inside it. She looked around for Katy, her favourite doll and placed her in the bag. She looked around again and spotted a jumper on the floor, so she picked it up, folded it up as best she could and placed that in the bag.

Thinking that she had all she needed Mandy crept quietly downstairs, being especially careful

135

when she reached the bottom in case she disturbed her mother. She looked around for her shoes, which had been put by the front door and crouched down to put them on. As she did so she suddenly felt uneasy, as if she was being watched. Slowly Mandy turned her head and realised that her mother was stood behind her. She felt a sickly feeling inside for she knew that she was surely going to suffer now.

Ruby stood leaning against the lounge door with a half empty glass of vodka in her hand and glared at her daughter.

"So you're off out then, are you?" she asked in a sarcastic manner.

"I…I was just…"

Mandy didn't have a chance to say anymore when her mother threw her glass at the wall, smashing it into hundreds of tiny pieces, before lunging at her, slapping her hard around the face. Mandy screamed, but that didn't stop her mother from picking her up by the waist and throwing her back onto the floor.

"Please don't hurt me Mummy," Mandy pleaded.

"Hurt you? You don't know the meaning of hurt. Going to run away from me, were you? And just how far did you think you were going to get?"

"I wasn't running away Mummy," sobbed Mandy, "I was just going to see Nanny." It was the first thing the poor little girl could think of to say, but as soon as she said it she knew it was the wrong answer.

"Oh so you think Nanny will help you, do you?" What have you been saying to dear old Nanny then?" Ruby reached forward as she spoke, grabbing the front of Mandy's jumper and pulling her up.

"Nothing, I haven't seen Nanny."

"Liar!" screamed Ruby as she slapped Mandy around the face again. "You saw her that day when your teacher took you over there. Getting very cosy with your Nanny and teachers, aren't you?"

"I didn't say anything, I promise," poor Mandy's eyes were streaming with tears as she put her hand up to her face where she had just been hit. Ruby grabbed her arm tightly and pulled her up the stairs. She opened the bedroom door and threw Mandy in the direction of her bed.

"Get in this room and stay there. If you can't be trusted not to try to escape then this is where you will have to stay from now on. Don't even think about trying to get away because I am going to lock every door in the house. If I so much as hear your door opening I will be up here so fast you won't know what's hit you. Do I make myself clear?"

"Yes Mummy," replied Mandy, still trembling with fear.

As she heard her mother's footsteps disappear down the stairs Mandy sat on her bed. She wiped away the tears with the back of her hands and looked around for a teddy. She spotted one on a windowsill and went over to fetch it. While at the window Mandy pulled back the net curtain and looked out, only just tall enough to see out properly. It was dusk outside, the night drawing in quickly. Mandy was glad she hadn't managed to run away because she didn't like the dark and would be frightened out there on her own. She put back the curtain, took off her clothes and put herself to bed. As she lifted the cover of the put-you-up bed the smell of stale urine wafted out. This didn't bother Mandy, she had become used to it by now, just as she had got used to getting into a damp bed. Clutching the teddy in her arms Mandy closed her eyes in an effort to get herself to sleep. This wasn't easy though, for she was worried about tomorrow. Mummy was going to be so cross when she found out what was going on and would surely punish her worse than ever before. Mandy thought of her father and the happy days she had spent with him and Mummy as a real family where nobody was ever cross or bad tempered. These thoughts seemed to comfort Mandy and she gradually drifted off to sleep.

Downstairs meanwhile, Ruby had gone straight back into the lounge, swearing as she stood on a piece of glass and cut the bottom of her foot. She managed to take out the tiny splinter of glass and threw it back on the ground in disgust. She then found an empty glass on the bar and poured herself fresh vodka. On her way back to the sofa Ruby glimpsed her wedding photo on the mantelpiece. She walked over and studied it for a few seconds, then raised her glass in front of it.

"Till death us do part," she quoted before taking a large sip from her glass, "Cheers Derek."

Ruby picked up the photo and placed it back face down on the mantelpiece before returning to the mini-bar and picking up the half empty vodka bottle, carrying it and the glass already in her hand back to the sofa. She was settled for the night. There was no reason for her to be disturbed now, after all there was only herself to look out for now. That was apart from the inconvenience of a five-year-old daughter who didn't seem to matter anymore.

Ruby sat back on the sofa, realising that the television was switched off. She swore as she struggled to get up and switch it on. As the screen flickered and came to life Ruby sat back down and finished off what was in her glass. There was a western film showing but Ruby wasn't really interested, all she wanted to do was drink her life away. She placed the empty glass back down on the coffee table and reached for the bottle. Taking a large swig she sighed and laid herself on the sofa, propping her head up with a pillow so that she could see the television. Every now and then she took another swig from the bottle until it was empty and she herself barely conscious. The film finished but Ruby was too far gone to notice. She just remained in her usual drunken state until the morning when she was woken up by the sound of her daughter trying to make some breakfast.

"Why the hell does that child have to make so much noise?" Ruby asked herself as she struggled to sit up. She sat still for a minute or so while the pounding in her head subsided slightly. Slowly she got up and headed for the kitchen. Mandy was just finishing her drink as she looked at her mother.

"What are you staring at?"

"Nothing Mummy," replied Mandy. As she put her cup down she knocked it over, spilling the last few drops onto the table.

"You clumsy little cow. Get out before I knock that stupid little head off its shoulders. I don't know why I ever had you; you're a waste of space!"

Mandy ran out of the back door and through the garden to the shed.

Back inside, Ruby picked up an empty vodka bottle and threw it at the wall, glass shattering everywhere. She then picked up her cigarettes and stormed up the stairs where she put herself to bed.

Chapter 12

Mandy looked around the shed and spotted a large spider in the corner on the floor. She didn't like spiders so she lifted her feet up on the chair and sat with her arms held tightly around her knees. She had spent many Saturday mornings in the shed but today was different. Today would turn out to be the Saturday that would change the course of her life. Many felt an uneasy feeling inside. Sooner or later she knew there would be a knock on the door, and Mummy would be really, really angry. Poor Mandy just sat, clutching her knees and rocking forward and backward on the chair, knowing that she couldn't stop whatever was going to happen later today. She closed her eyes and began to think of her Father, and before long she began softly speaking to him…

"Daddy, if you're watching me from Heaven, please don't let them make Mummy angry. Please make them not come so Mummy won't tell me off. Please Daddy; I know Mummy doesn't mean to hurt me. Don't let them come and take me away 'cos Mummy will be all alone and sad." The tears welled up in Mandy's eyes as she spoke, "I better go now and see if Mummy's okay."

She wiped her eyes on the back of her hands and climbed down from the chair and out of the shed, closing the door behind her. Very carefully and as quietly as she could Mandy opened the back door and crept into the kitchen. There was no sign of her mother so the little girl crept over to the lounge door, peering in, but there was still no sign.

"She must be in bed," Mandy thought, so she made her way up the stairs to her own bedroom. At the top of the stairs she paused, noticing that her mother's bedroom door was open. As quietly as she could Mandy took a couple of steps towards the door and looked in, suddenly startled by her mother's voice.

"What are you looking at?" Ruby asked sharply. She was sat up in bed with a cigarette in one hand and the other supporting an ashtray.

"N..nothing, I just wondered where you were."

"Well you've found me now, was there something you wanted?"

"No Mummy."

"Well piss off then, and shut the door behind you," shouted Ruby as she took a last drag from her cigarette and stubbed it out in the ashtray. She put the ashtray down on the bedside cabinet and lay down, burying her head under the covers.

Mandy did as she was told and closed the door behind her. She walked across to her own bedroom and found her dolls. The little girl played for an hour or so until she got bored with her dolls and decided to go downstairs to see what was on the television. By now it was almost midday and Mandy realised she was hungry, so headed for the kitchen.

As she reached the hallway Mandy heard footsteps coming towards the front door. Her heart almost skipped a beat and she suddenly felt sick. This was the moment she had been dreading.

The doorbell rang and Mandy froze on the spot. What should she do? The bell rang again and Mandy heard her mother's voice from upstairs.

"Whoever that is, tell them to come back later."

Mandy was shaking uncontrollably by now, unable to move from the spot. The bell rang again, accompanied by a loud knock on the door.

"For Christ's sake, where is that girl?" came the voice from upstairs. The sound of her mother coming downstairs seemed to break the spell and Mandy ran from the spot where she was stood, straight out of the back door to the shed. She climbed back onto the chair and into the same crouched position as before.

"Please make them go away," pleaded Mandy to herself as she rocked to and fro on the chair. She was terrified.

Back inside the house Ruby managed to make her way downstairs, wrapping her dressing gown tightly around her. She opened the front door.

"Mrs Croft?" asked one of the two people stood in front of her.

"Yes, who's asking?" replied Ruby abruptly.

My name is Mr Lawrence and this is my colleague, Miss Diane Parkes. We are from the Social Services Department and are acting on information we have received concerning the welfare of your daughter, Mandy."

"What information? I've had a visit from Social Services before and they closed the case because they could find nothing wrong. Has my mother-in-law been in touch with you again? She has nothing better to do than to cause trouble for me."

"Actually it wasn't your mother-in-law. May we please come in and discuss the matter?"

Ruby panicked. She knew what state the house was in; there had been no warning this time so she couldn't hide the evidence.

"Could you possibly come back in an hour? As you can see I'm not dressed yet."

"I'm sorry Mrs Croft, but we need to come in now, replied Mr Lawrence sternly. "There are serious concerns regarding your daughter which require our immediate attention."

Ruby stepped back, allowing the two Social Workers to enter, knowing that any resistance would make matters worse. Diane entered first, followed by her superior. They gave each other a knowing glance as the smell hit them. It was a mixture of alcohol, nicotine and rotting rubbish. Ruby led them into the kitchen where she offered them both a seat at the table before pulling herself a chair out.

"Please excuse the mess, I've not been well lately and have got a bit behind with the housework."
Mr Lawrence ignored the remark and got straight to the point.

"Mrs Croft," he began, opening a file that he had placed on the table in front of him. "It has come to our attention that there may be signs of physical abuse on Mandy."

"What do you mean 'physical abuse'? I love my daughter dearly. She's everything to me. Why on earth would I want to hurt her?"

"Mrs Croft, there have been several occasions when your daughter has gone to school with cuts and bruises which, when asked about them she has seemed reluctant to say how they occurred."

"So my daughter's gone to school with a few cuts and bruises. Isn't that normal for a five year old? I know when I was her age I was always falling over and getting into scrapes."

"As you say, the odd bruise or graze is normal for a young child, but when a happy child becomes withdrawn and frightened to talk to a teacher, and has fresh marks almost every day then there is a cause for concern."

"This is ridiculous. Why would I want to hurt my daughter?"

"Mrs Croft we are not accusing you of anything but we do have to see for ourselves based on any evidence we may have."

"What evidence?" Ruby was becoming very agitated by now. "You have no evidence. All you're doing is going by hearsay from a couple of teachers who think they can poke their noses into other peoples' business."

It was Diane who spoke next.

"Mrs Croft, is Mandy home?"

"Yes she is, why?"

"We will need to talk to her."

"Why? You lot spoke to her before and she told you she was very happy here. Why do you need to question her again?"

"We need to be sure," Mr Lawrence answered, "now please could you get Mandy for us?"

"Very well, although I think you're wasting your time. She's in her bedroom, I'll go and fetch her." Ruby stood up and headed upstairs calling to Mandy, but there was no answer from the little girl's bedroom. Ruby opened the door and realised the room was empty.

"Shit," she uttered under her breath as she turned and headed back down the stairs. She straightened her dressing gown before entering the kitchen again.

"She's not up there, she must be out in the garden."

"We'll help you look," said Diane as both Social Workers stood up.

"I'll just look in the lounge," suggested Mr Lawrence as he headed out of the kitchen. As he opened the lounge door he looked around. The curtains were still drawn, but this didn't stop him from seeing the state of the room and smelling the mixture of stale ashtrays and alcohol. He walked back to where the two women were stood in the kitchen.

"Any sign?" asked Diane.

"No, she must be outside," replied her colleague. Ruby opened the back door and the three adults stepped outside.

146

Inside the shed Mandy was still sat on the chair. She was hoping that her mother had managed to make the people go away. She would still be very angry but sooner or later she would calm down and then things would be back to normal, or at least what had now become normal for Mandy and her mother.

The silence in the shed was suddenly interrupted by the sound of Ruby's voice calling her daughter. It sounded unusually cheerful, which seemed to put Mandy's mind at ease, prompting her to climb down from the chair to see what her mum wanted.

"Yes Mummy?" she asked as she opened the shed door. Mandy's heart sank as she saw the two people stood outside the shed with her mother. The time had come. At this moment poor Mandy wished that she could become invisible, never to be seen again; but she knew in her own innocent way that she was going to have to tell the truth about Mummy, even if it meant she could no longer stay with her. She bowed her head to the ground and walked slowly over to where the three adults stood.

"Hello Mandy," said Diane as she held her hand out to the little girl, "we've come to see how you and your Mummy are coping."

Mandy lightly grasped Diane's hand. She somehow felt safe, knowing that these people were here to help her.

"Shall we go inside?" asked Mr Lawrence turning towards Mandy, "It's a bit chilly out here and you've still got your nightclothes on."

147

"That's a good idea, isn't it sweetie?" answered Ruby, trying to sound like the caring mother that she once was. She led everyone back into the kitchen where the three adults returned to their seats. Mandy stood shyly, unsure of what she should do next. Diane spotted the worried look on Mandy's face and tried to reassure her.

"Don't worry Darling, you're not in any kind of trouble, we're just here to make sure that you and Mummy are managing. Why don't you go upstairs to your bedroom and play for a while? I'll be up shortly to have a chat with you."

"Okay," replied Mandy and did as she was asked. She smiled sweetly at the young Social Worker before heading out of the kitchen. Diane seemed somehow affected by that smile; it was as if a connection had just been made between the two of them. Although the Social Worker had seen many children in the three years she had been with the department, none of them had instantly struck a chord in the was this little girl had just done. Diane paused for a second before composing herself and turned back to Ruby and Mr Lawrence, who was re-opening the file in front of him. He flicked through the pages until he found the section he was looking for then turned to Ruby.

"Mrs Croft, as I have said already we are here because we have received information which is rather concerning."

"And as I have said already, you're wasting your time." Ruby was finding it extremely difficult to hold her temper and she desperately needed a drink. Her hands were shaking, partly from anger but mostly from the effects of her alcoholism.

"May we have a look around your house?" asked Mr Lawrence.

"What the hell for, evidence that I'm beating my child?"

"Mrs Croft, please calm down. We are only doing our jobs and shouting isn't going to get us anywhere," said Diane, softly but sternly.

"Go ahead look around, I've nothing to hide." Ruby sat back in her chair with her legs outstretched and arms folded.

"Thank you," replied Mr Lawrence as he picked up the file and put his hand in his pocket to take out a pen. Both Social Workers looked around the kitchen, occasionally giving each other knowing glances. The worktops were in the usual untidy state, empty bread wrappers left out with three or four mouldy slices remaining, a half empty milk bottle which had obviously been there for a number of days, and a sink full of dirty crockery which was piling up over the draining board. The rubbish bin had overflowed so much that the area of floor around it was covered with waste food and tins. Mr Lawrence began making notes, much to Ruby's annoyance.

"What are you writing?" she asked rudely.

"I need to make notes Mrs Croft, so that I can assess the situation and pass any information to my Officer-in-charge."

"What information. Have you never seen a messy kitchen before?"

The two Social Workers carried on with their observations, ignoring Ruby's interjections. Once finished in the kitchen they headed for the lounge, closely followed by Ruby. Diane went straight to the window to open the curtains while her colleague began writing more notes. The main topic in this room was the amount of empty vodka bottles that were lying around, along with overfull ashtrays, the contents of which had scattered all over the coffee table and carpet below. There was a very stuffy smell in this room; Diane wanted to open the window but avoided the temptation. Instead she stood waiting for her colleague to finish writing his notes.

"May we please go up and talk to your daughter, Mrs Croft?" asked Mr Lawrence as he finished writing.

"Anything you have to say to her you can say in front of me. How do I know what kind of rubbish you might put into her head?" replied Ruby defensively.

"Okay Mrs Croft. We can talk to Mandy with you present, but if we suspect that she feels intimidated by you then we do have the right to speak to her alone."

"I'll go and get her," agreed Ruby, realising that she couldn't let the Social Workers see her daughter's bedroom.

"It's okay, we'll go up to her," suggested Diane, "If she's up there playing then there's no point in disturbing her any more than we have to."

Before Ruby could stop them the two Social Workers were half way up the stairs. As they reached the top Mr Lawrence turned to Ruby.

"Is this the one?" he asked, pointing to the first door they came to.

"Yes," replied Ruby, curtly.

Mr Lawrence knocked and turned the handle. As the door opened a smell of stale urine escaped, causing him to step back for a second. Diane and Ruby were close behind him.

"Hello Mandy, may we come in?" asked Diane. Mandy gave that smile again, causing the young social worker to feel an overwhelming compassion for her. Mandy saw her mum enter the room and bowed her head down to the floor. The two social workers noticed this but said nothing.

"What are you doing?" asked Diane as she knelt down beside Mandy.

"Playing with my dolls," Mandy answered in a barely audible voice.

"Do they have names?"

"This one's Katy, she's my favourite," replied Mandy as she picked up the doll and handed it to Diane.

"She's lovely. Do you play with your dollies a lot?"

"Yes, every day when Mummy's asleep." Many looked towards her mother who was staring at her. Immediately she put her head down, realising she had probably just said the wrong thing. Ruby had to think quickly now.

"I have a little nap in the afternoons. You know how it is when you have kids; I just need half hour or so to recharge my batteries and then I'm right as rain. Isn't that right sweetie?" Ruby looked at her daughter, prompting her to answer.

"Yes Mummy."

"I hear you started school recently; do you enjoy it there?" asked Diane as she gave the doll back to Mandy.

"Yes," came the reply quietly. Mandy glanced at her mother and looked down again. Diane sensed the nervousness of the little girl and looked at her colleague. He immediately knew what that meant and turned to Ruby.

"Mrs Croft, I think it would be better if we spoke to Mandy on her own, would you mind waiting downstairs?"

"Actually I do mind. This is my house and my daughter. She's five years old, what can she possibly say that would be of any use to you?"

"Mrs Croft, please. It will be better for all concerned if you could co-operate with us. Diane will be here so you can be sure Mandy won't be made to tell us anything she doesn't want to."

"Don't have a lot of choice really, do I?" groaned Ruby as she stormed out of the room. Mr Lawrence waited to hear Ruby's footsteps going down the stairs and closed the bedroom door. He looked around the room, still holding open the file, and started to jot down notes about the state of Mandy's bedroom. As he looked around he saw the put-you-up bed, the blanket pulled back just enough to reveal the stained mattress underneath. He didn't need to touch it, he could see how wet it still was. In the corner of the room was a pile of dirty clothes, which Mandy had folded as neatly as possible. The rest of the room was reasonably tidy but there was no escaping the stench of stale urine. Mr Lawrence opened the window to let some fresh air into the room before moving a teddy bear from a chair and sitting in it himself. Meanwhile, Diane began to speak softly to Mandy.

"Mandy darling, please don't be worried. We need to ask you a few questions but if you feel you can't answer then that's fine, just do the best you can."

"Okay," came the little voice. With her mother absent, Mandy seemed a little more at ease.

"Mandy," began Diane, "Are you happy living here with Mummy?"

"Yes," came the reply albeit somewhat hesitantly.

"You're not worried about anything are you?"

"No."

Diane reached out to take Mandy's hand. As the little girl put hers out the social worker spotted the scar. Without giving away the fact she had seen it she held Mandy's hand and spoke reassuringly.

"Mandy, your teacher has spoken to us and she is very worried about you. She says that you don't seem as happy as you did when you first started at school and are very quiet in class. Your friends are worried about you too; they say that you fall over a lot at home but don't tell them how it happens. There was one time when you had a nasty cut on your chin, but when they asked about it you got upset and ran away."

153

"I fell off a chair," came the reply rather quickly.

"That's okay Mandy, accidents happen. Can you tell me why you were climbing on a chair though?"

"I...I was trying to get a drink and I slipped."

"Wouldn't it have been easier to ask Mummy to get you a drink?"

"She was asleep and I didn't want to wake her."

"Does Mummy sleep a lot?"

"Yes, but I don't mind. She gets bad heads so I have to leave her to sleep."

"Has Mummy been to the doctor about her bad heads?"

"I don't know."

"That's okay Mandy, don't worry," said Diane, realising that Mandy was becoming tense. She decided to change the subject slightly.

"Mandy, your teacher is a bit worried that you don't bring your packed lunch into school. Do you forget to bring it in?"

"I...I don't know how to make it; but it doesn't matter 'cause Mrs Albright always asks the class if they have any spare to share with me."

"Mandy, does Mummy get up with you in the mornings and help you get ready for school?"

"No. She says I'm five and that's old enough to get myself ready and walk to school."

"Do you mean you walk to school on your own?" Diane looked across to her colleague, finding it hard to believe what she was hearing. He gave a concerned look back.

154

Mandy nodded, fearing she had given too much information. Diane took a deep breath before asking the next question.

"Mandy that mark on your hand; can you tell me how you got it?"
The little girl pulled her hand away from the social worker's and covered it with her dressing-gown sleeve.

"Please Mandy, I know you're worried but we really are here to help you."

"I...I can't tell you." The little girl began to cry. Diane put her arm around her and spoke softly.

"Why can't you tell us, Mandy?"

"Mummy will shout at me," she sobbed.

"Why will she shout at you, darling?" asked Diane, holding Mandy tighter.

"It was my fault. I wet myself so it was my fault. Please don't say anything to Mummy or she will get cross."

"Mandy, we won't say anything to Mummy, but you must understand that your Mummy needs help, and the only way to help her is by knowing everything that has happened. If there is anything else please tell us, it will all work out for the best in the end."

"She doesn't mean to do it; it's just that water she drinks. It makes her cross but she says she needs it 'cause I'm such a handful."
Diane looked at her colleague. They both knew that Mandy had had enough of being questioned. The poor girl looked terrified. Mr Lawrence finished writing his notes and looked at Mandy.

"Well done young lady. I know it hasn't been easy but things will get better. Diane and I will be back later to see you and Mummy but until then please don't worry."

Mandy looked at Diane, who also reassured her before the two social workers stood up and made their way out of the room. Diane glanced back and gave Mandy a warm smile. Mandy smiled back.

Downstairs, Ruby was in the kitchen, finishing a cigarette. She quickly stubbed it out in an ashtray and stood up to greet the social workers.

"Well, gather any useful information?" she asked, sarcastically.

"Mrs Croft," replied Mr Lawrence, "Miss Parkes and I have spoken to Mandy but we need to make reports on our findings and return when a satisfactory conclusion has been decided."

"What in hell does that mean?"

"It means, Mrs Croft, that there are issues which need to be addressed and we will be in touch in due course."

"What issues? There are no issues. The only problem we have are nosey do-gooders who have nothing better to do than to stick their noses into other peoples' business." Ruby was becoming quite agitated.

"We will return soon, Mrs Croft. We'll let ourselves out," said Mr Lawrence. Ruby followed them to the front door without speaking and closed it hard behind them. She stormed into the lounge, cursing under her breath.

"I need a drink!" she announced and headed for the mini-bar. Then she remembered that she was out of vodka, with no money to buy more.

"Shit!" she shouted as she looked on the bar for something else to drink. She spotted a full bottle of Derek's favourite whisky and grabbed it, unscrewing the lid quickly. She didn't like whisky but was desperate for a drink. She took a large swig of the liquid, almost choking as the liquor burned the back of her throat.

Ruby looked around and found herself a glass to pour some of the whisky into. With the glass in her hand she made her way upstairs to Mandy's room. As the door opened Mandy's heart began racing. She knew Mummy would be really cross.

"So, what has Mummy's little sweetie been saying about her then?"

"Nothing Mummy."

"Are you sure? You wouldn't want me to get angry now, would you?"

"No Mummy, but I didn't say anything," replied Mandy, absolutely terrified.

"Well they've gone now so they couldn't have been that worried, could they?
I'm going back to bed, and if anyone knocks on the door for God's sake, don't answer it. Do you think you can manage that?"

"Yes Mummy."

Ruby walked out of the room and into her own bedroom, leaving little Mandy surprised but relieved that she wasn't going to get a beating. Mandy remained in her room, playing with her dolls while Ruby put herself to bed, not before gulping down the whisky in the glass, and fell asleep.

Chapter 13

Mandy was confused. Mrs Wade had told her that these people would help her. So why had they been and gone again without doing anything? Perhaps it was normal after all for her mother to shout at her and hit her the way she did; perhaps it was normal to make her survive on whatever scraps of food were left in the kitchen. She was thankful, however that her mother hadn't got really cross with her. Ruby had become so unpredictable lately that anything could have happened.

Mandy dragged her chair over to the window and kneeled up on it, looking out to the street below. Outside some young girls were pushing dolls' prams along the road. Mandy longed to be out there with the children, but Mummy didn't want her mixing with them. She said they were 'trouble-makers' and couldn't be trusted. Instead Mandy had to amuse herself with the few dolls and toys that she had. She felt very lonely at times, and would often lie on her bed and drift off to sleep just to make the day go quicker. It was only at school that she had any contact with the outside world.

After half an hour or so Mandy climbed down from the window and very quietly made her way downstairs, careful not to disturb her mother who was by now in a deep sleep. She was hungry; after all it was late afternoon by now and she had eaten nothing all day, so she made her way into the kitchen to see if there was anything worth eating in there. After looking around Mandy realised there was nothing so she made her way outside to the shed where she knew there was a biscuit left in her secret box. It was fairly cold outside, being late October. The nights were really drawing in early and within an hour or so it would be dark. Mandy ate her biscuit and went back indoors. It was much too cold for her to stay outside, especially as she still had her nightclothes on. Once back in the kitchen, Mandy climbed up on a chair in front of the sink, found a glass and poured herself some water from the tap. Carefully she climbed down and dragged the chair over to the table where she sat with her glass of water.

The silence in the house was suddenly broken by the sound of the doorbell. Mandy put down her glass and just sat, remembering that Mummy had told her not to answer the door. The bell rang again and Mandy crept quietly to the kitchen door, from where she could see the front door. The letterbox opened and Mandy could just about make out the face of Diane peering through. The Social Worker spotted the little girl and spoke softly.

"Mandy, could you open the door?" Mandy looked towards the top of the stairs to see if there was any sign of her mother. She couldn't hear or see anything so she walked slowly towards the front door. She looked at the letterbox which was just about head height.

"Mummy said not to let anyone in," she whispered, afraid of making too much noise and waking Mummy up.

"Where is Mummy?" asked Diane, still holding open the letterbox.

"She's in bed."

The little girl was scared. She didn't know what to do for the best. They had come back to help her, but if she opened the door then Mummy would be cross. On the other hand, if she didn't then Diane would go away and might not come back again to help her. Diane closed the letterbox and turned to her colleague.

"I think we should go round and see if the back door's open, that poor little girl is scared."

"I agree," replied Mr Lawrence, "I'll just go and let the police know what's happening.

He walked back down the front path to the gate where two police officers were waiting. They had been called to assist the two social workers in case of any problems. The two officers accompanied them as they made their way around the side of the house to the back door. One of the officers turned the handle and the door opened.

Mr Lawrence entered first, followed by his colleague and then the police. There was no sign of anybody in the kitchen so the four adults walked into the hallway. Mandy had heard the back door open and had run upstairs to her bedroom. She grabbed Katy and clutched the doll tightly in her arms while sitting on the edge of her bed. She sat and listened to the social workers as they called out.

"Mrs Croft!" shouted Mr Lawrence as he opened the lounge door and looked in. There was no sign. He made his way up the stairs followed by

Diane, while the two police officers remained at the bottom of the stairs.

Once they had reached the landing Diane knocked quietly before opening Mandy's bedroom door. The little girl looked up.

"Are you okay Mandy?"

"Yes."

"Please don't worry darling, come downstairs with me."

"But what about Mummy?"

"Don't worry about Mummy for the moment. We'll wake her up and once she's downstairs we all need to have a little talk."

"What's going to happen?"

"Let's just get you downstairs. Don't worry, everything will be alright."

Diane held out her hand to Mandy and led her downstairs into the lounge. The two police officers had moved into the kitchen by then but Mandy spotted them from the hallway.

"Why are they here?" She asked.

"They were just here to make sure we could get into the house, nothing to worry about," answered Diane as she led Mandy into the lounge.

Meanwhile, upstairs Mr Lawrence opened Ruby's bedroom door and stood in the doorway.

"Mrs Croft!" he called quite loudly.

Ruby stirred.

"Mrs Croft!"

This time Ruby sat upright when she heard the male voice in her room.

"What the hell are you doing in my house?" she shouted, looking down to make sure she was adequately covered up.

"The back door was open. I did tell you we would return, Mrs Croft. Could you please get up? I will be in the lounge with my colleague when you're ready."

Mr Lawrence turned to exit the room.

"Bloody do-gooders. You've nothing better to do than poke your noses where they're not wanted. Why don't you just get lost, and take your snotty girlfriend with you?"

"When you're ready please, Mrs Croft." The social worker made his way downstairs where one of the police officers was waiting in the hallway.

"Everything okay?" he asked.

"Yes, she'll be down in a minute. I think we may need your assistance in a while though, I have a feeling this won't be easy."

"Okay, we'll be in the kitchen until needed."

"Thanks," replied Mr Lawrence as he walked into the lounge.

"Mummy will be down in a few minutes," said the social worker to Mandy, "try not to worry."

"Okay," she replied, but both adults could see the worried look on her face.

Upstairs, Ruby sat on the edge of her bed. She knew they were coming back but this was ridiculous. It couldn't have been more than an hour or so since they had left earlier. What could be so urgent that they had to barge into her house uninvited and wake her up? She put her hands to her head, the throbbing almost unbearable. After a

163

couple of minutes Ruby took a deep breath and stood up, straightening her dressing gown. Her head was really pounding; the whisky seemed to have had a worse effect than the usual vodka.

"Right, here goes," she uttered under her breath as she made her way downstairs. She didn't see the police in the kitchen as she headed for the lounge.

The lounge door was already slightly ajar so Ruby pushed it open enough to walk in. Mr Lawrence was on one of the armchairs, while Diane was sat on the sofa with Mandy perched close to her.

"Mrs Croft," said Mr Lawrence, "Thank you for coming down. I'll get straight to the point: a decision has been made regarding your daughter and the present situation."

"What decision?" asked Ruby as she sat on the remaining armchair.

"Mrs Croft, we feel that under the circumstances it would be unwise for Mandy to remain with you."

"What are you talking about? Are you saying that I can't look after my own daughter?"

"What we are saying is that we feel Mandy would be better off in the care of Social Services. We have obtained an emergency care order and once the courts are open on Monday we will be applying for a proper court order."

"I don't believe this! You can't take my daughter away from me, I've done nothing wrong!" Ruby stood up and stormed over to where Mandy was sitting and grabbed her by the arm. Diane tried to pull Ruby away but she had a really tight grip on her daughter's arm. Mandy screamed as she was pulled away from the social worker.

"Mrs Croft, please!" shouted Mr Lawrence, You're upsetting your daughter."

"You're the ones upsetting her, not me! Go away and leave us alone, we're fine without you." Ruby held Mandy tightly; there was no way that anyone was going to take her away.

From the kitchen the police heard the commotion and rushed into the lounge. Ruby was surprised to see them but it didn't stop her holding on for dear life to her daughter.

"Please, Mrs Croft," said one of the officers, "let's all just calm down. Can't you see there's a child here who's very upset and frightened?"

"I'll calm down when you get these people out of my house," shouted Ruby, almost hysterically.

"Please let Mandy go," pleaded Diane, "you're not doing yourself any favours by acting this way."

Ruby released her grip and Mandy ran to the social worker. Diane knelt down to her level and put her arms around her. The tears were streaming down Mandy's face as she clung tightly to the social worker's coat.

"It's okay darling, everything's going to be alright. You're safe now."

The police officers led Ruby out into the hallway, where they managed to calm her down slightly. She seemed to realise that she was in a no-win situation. If she shouted it made things worse than they already were, but if she said nothing they were still going to take Mandy away. After a couple of minutes Mr Lawrence came out of the lounge to speak to Ruby.

"Mrs Croft, I know it's difficult but you must see that it's for the best. You need help and Mandy needs to be somewhere she can feel safe. I will give you a chance to say goodbye, but please don't do anything silly, it will just make matters worse for yourself."

"Where are you taking her?"

"We will be in touch in due course to let you know where Mandy is, but I think it is probably better that you have a couple of days to calm down and reflect."

"You can't just take her away and not tell me where she's going. She's my daughter!" Ruby was becoming agitated again. She tried to go back into the lounge but the police were too quick, holding her back.

"Mrs Croft, could you please wait in the kitchen while we get some of Mandy's things together?" asked Mr Lawrence.

The police led her into the kitchen and closed the door while the social worker went back into the lounge where his colleague was waiting with Mandy.

"Where's Mummy?" asked Mandy.

"She's in the kitchen at the moment; don't worry about her, she'll be fine."

Mr Lawrence sat back on the chair and turned towards Mandy.

"Now then Mandy, do you think you could go upstairs with Diane and show her where your clothes are? You need to get dressed before we leave."

"Where are we going?"

"Diane is going to take you to a place not far from here where you will be looked after for the time being."

"But I don't want to go, I can't leave Mummy on her own," Mandy cried. After everything she had been through she still couldn't bear to see Mummy upset.

"It's okay Mandy. There really is no need to worry," said Diane, trying to comfort the little girl. She had been in this situation before with other children, but whatever the circumstances it was never easy separating a child from their parents. She held out her hand and Mandy took it, both of them leaving the room and heading upstairs to Mandy's bedroom.

"Right then, can you show me where you keep your clean clothes?" asked the social worker as she went to open the chest of drawers.

"There's no clean clothes left, Mummy hasn't washed any for a long time."

"Okay," Diane answered, trying not to sound surprised, "What about this?" she asked, holding up a dress that had been folded neatly on the floor. She could see that it hadn't been washed but it was still wearable for the time being.

"But that one's dirty," answered Mandy.

"I'll tell you what, if you can make do with this one just for tonight then on Monday morning I

167

will take you out and we'll go into town to look for some new clothes for you. How does that sound?"

"Can I choose anything I want?"

"Of course you can darling, and we'll buy a few more bits that you may need, okay?"
Mandy took off her dressing gown and nightie with the help of Diane, and then put on the dress.

"Where are your shoes, Mandy?" asked the social worker.

"Downstairs by the front door."

"Come on then, let's go and find them. Oh, I nearly forgot, are there any toys that you would like to take with you?"

"Only Katy," replied Mandy as she picked up the doll.
The two of them headed downstairs, put Mandy's shoes on and back into the lounge where Mr Lawrence was waiting.

"You just wait here darling and I'll just go and see if Mummy's ready to say goodbye," said Diane.
Both social workers left the lounge, closing the door behind them. They paused in the hallway to speak.

"That poor girl's got no clean clothes so I'll sort that on Monday. The main thing is we get her to Whiteways."

"I agree, time's getting on and the first thing she's going to need is a bath and a good meal. Come on, let's get this over with."
Diane returned to the lounge while Mr Lawrence opened the kitchen door. Ruby was sat calmly at the table with the two police officers. She sat upright in anticipation as the social worker spoke.

"Mrs Croft, Mandy is ready to go now. Please don't make this any harder for her, she's anxious and really doesn't need to be upset anymore."

"I'll do my best, although I've done nothing to deserve this." Ruby stood up and made her way into the lounge, closely followed by Mr Lawrence with the police waiting in the hallway. Mandy was sat on Diane' knee.

"I'm so sorry, sweetie," said Ruby as she walked towards her daughter. Mandy got down from Diane's lap and ran at her mother, giving her the biggest hug she could.

"That's okay Mummy. Please don't be sad." The tears were streaming down Ruby's face. What had she done to this poor, sweet little girl? She hugged her tightly, not wanting to let go. Diane looked on, unable to stop her own tears. She reached into her pocket for a tissue and wiped her eyes before putting her hand on Mandy's shoulder.

"Come on darling, it's time to go." Mandy loosened her grip, leaving a wet patch on her mother's chest where she too had been crying.

"Go on sweetheart, and you be good for Mummy, you hear?"

"Yes Mummy," replied Mandy as she took Diane' hand.

"Don't forget Katy," said Diane as she picked up the doll and handed it to Mandy. The little girl grabbed the doll with her free hand and followed the social worker into the hallway. She turned to her mother who was close behind.

"Bye Mummy," she said, trying to be brave and not cry again.

"Bye, sweetheart," replied Ruby, the lump in her throat getting bigger all the time. Diane led Mandy out of the house to her own car, which was parked just outside. Once in the car Mandy could see Mr Lawrence talking to her mother, although she couldn't hear what was being said. She watched as he left the house and walked over to his car, which was parked across the road. The police also left at the same time.

Diane started the engine and turned to Mandy.

"Are you alright?"

"Yes, thank you," answered Mandy as she looked back towards her mother.

The car pulled away and Mandy waved. Ruby stood at the doorway and waved back, unable to stop the floods of tears. Once the car was out of sight Ruby entered the house closing the door behind her. She went into the kitchen, pulled out a chair and sat at the table with her head buried in her arms.

Ruby cried and cried, unable to stop. What had she done? She had lost the one person that meant anything to her, although for the last few months she had treated her appallingly. After a long while Ruby lifted her head up and looked around the kitchen. She spotted an empty glass on the side and picked it up. She then carried it out of the kitchen and into the lounge where she had put the whiskey bottle earlier. She opened the bottle and poured a measure of the liquid into the glass before sitting down on the sofa. Ruby closed her eyes and took a large gulp from the glass. The liquid burned as it hit her throat but that didn't stop her from taking another gulp. She sat back and looked up at the fireplace where she spotted the photo of her wedding day. She held the glass up in the direction of the photo and spoke.

"I'm so sorry Derek, please forgive me." Ruby poured another drink into the glass and gulped it down as quickly as the first two, before lying down on the sofa and drifting into a deep sleep.

In the car Mandy was very quiet. What was going to happen now? Diane sensed her anxiousness and began to talk softly to her.

"Mandy please don't worry. The place where you're going has lots of other children just like you to play with. They all have different problems which mean that for one reason or another they can't live at home, so they come to live at this place while we try to sort out what's best for them."

"Is there a Mummy and Daddy where I'm going?"

"No, but there are people who look after you every day, just like a Mummy or a Daddy. They don't all look after you at the same time because they have families of their own to look after, so they share the time that they look after you."

"Are the other children nice?"

"I'm sure you'll get on really well with the children Mandy. There are boys and girls of different ages and I'm sure you'll find someone to play with very soon."

"I'm not playing with boys, they're yuk!" said Mandy.

Diane laughed.

"What's so funny?" asked Mandy innocently.

"Nothing, nothing at all. I'm sure you'll find some girls to play with."

They drove a couple of miles before Diane slowed the car down and turned into a long driveway.

"Here we are, Whiteways."

Mandy leaned forward in her seat to see out of the windscreen. The driveway was lined with tall trees. As she looked in front of her, Mandy saw the most enormous house she had ever seen.

"Wow! Is this it?"

"It sure is," answered Diane as she parked the car just outside the main entrance, "Are you ready to see your new home?"

Chapter 14

Mandy quickly became nervous. She waited for Diane to open her door before climbing out of the car. She stood for a moment looking up at a large house. It was huge! It was an old stone building, most of it covered in ivy. The lead windows made it look to Mandy a bit like a castle, and because it was almost dark she thought it looked a bit spooky so she grabbed Diane's hand for comfort. To the left of the building Mandy could just make out what looked like a large field.

"That's where the children play outside when the weather's nice; sometimes they even have picnics out there."

"I used to have picnics in the garden with Mummy," replied Mandy. She put her head down as she suddenly remembered that she had left Mummy all on her own. "She will be okay won't she?"

"Of course she will, darling. Now come on, it's cold out here. Let's go inside."

Diane led Mandy to the front door and rang the bell. It was an old-fashioned musical bell which seemed to chime forever, and no sooner as it stopped the door opened. A small lady stood in front of Diane and Mandy. She must have been in her late fifties, with grey hair tied loosely back. Over a floral dress she wore a white apron, stained with gravy. She was holding a tea-towel in her hand.

"Hello, you must be Mandy," said the old lady in a cheerful voice, which instantly put the little girl at ease. "Come on in, out of the cold."

Diane gently prompted Mandy to enter the large hallway of the house. She stepped inside and looked around in amazement. The hall was bigger than her lounge at home, with large gold framed pictures hung neatly on the walls. Immediately in front of them was a large stairway, covered with a deep red carpet.

To the left of the stairway was a door, which suddenly burst open. A small red-haired boy ran out, almost tripping over his own feet. He saw the old lady an immediately slowed his pace.

"Where are you off to in such a hurry, Jonathon Norris?" asked the old lady.

"To the toilet, Miss."

"Well hurry up then, but straight back to finish your tea please."

"Yes Miss," replied Jonathon with a mischievous grin. He walked out of the hallway and through another door, disappearing along a passageway.

"Sorry about that. Now then, where were we? Oh yes, I haven't introduced myself yet, have I? My name is Rosemary, but most of the children call me Rose or Miss. It's up to you really, I don't mind either way."

Diane turned to Rose.

"Can I leave this young lady in your capable hands? I'm sure she's dying to get settled and meet the other children."

"Yes of course. We'll be just fine, won't we Mandy?"

"Yes." Replied the little girl nervously. Diane knelt down to her level and took hold of her hand.

"Rose will look after you now, Darling. I'll see you on Monday morning about 10 o'clock so we can go out and buy those clothes and things you need. It's been a long day so I expect you'll sleep well tonight. Bye for now."

"Bye," said Mandy as she watched the two adults say their goodbyes. Rose closed the door and turned to Mandy.

"Right, here we are then. You look like you need a good meal inside you, young lady. Why don't I take you up to your bedroom, then you can have a lovely soak in the bath before I find you something to eat?"

"Okay," Mandy replied as she followed Rose up the large staircase. At the top of the stairs were two doors, one on the left and one on the right.

"That side is where the boys sleep," pointed Rose to the door on the left, "and this is where the girls sleep." She opened the door on the right and held it for Mandy to enter. They were now at the beginning of a long corridor, with five doors leading from it; two on the right and three on the left. Rose stopped at the first door on the right.

"This is where Anna and Sarah sleep. They're sisters and they've been with us for about a year now," said Rose as she opened the door for Mandy to look in. The room was very neat, with two single beds positioned next to each other. They each had a navy cover on them with an assortment of teddies on top. Rose closed the door and opened the one opposite.

"This is where Joanna sleeps. She's fifteen and the oldest of all the children here."
Mandy looked in. The walls were adorned with posters of the latest pop stars, the rest of the room was a typical teenagers' room, with clothes strewn all over the floor, the bed left un-made and make up left out on the dressing table.

"I thought I'd asked her to tidy up this mess. Never mind, she can do it after tea," said Rose as she shut the door and led Mandy to the next room on the left.

"This one's the girls' bathroom; I'll show you that in a moment."
Rose walked a bit further, followed closely by Mandy. She opened the next door on the left.

"This is where Susan and Ruth sleep. Susan's twelve and Ruth's thirteen. They're best friends and do everything together. Sometimes we have a job separating them," laughed Rose as she held the door long enough for Mandy to look inside. As with Anna and Sarah's room this one was neat and tidy, the only difference was that this one had bunk beds instead of two single beds. Rose closed the door and turned to the last remaining door in the corridor.

"And last but not least, this one is your room."
Mandy looked inside from the doorway, unsure whether or not to go in.

"You can go in Sweetie, it's your room," reassured Rose, "you'll be sharing with Sophie.

She's six years old and she's only been with us for a few weeks. I'm sure you'll both become good friends."

Mandy looked around the room. The beds were positioned next to each other, both with the same matching blue covers. Above one of the beds were posters and pictures, and on the bed various cuddly toys and dolls.

The other half of the room looked bare. The bed was neatly made but there were no teddies or posters, and the bedside cabinet was empty.

"I know it's all a bit strange at the moment, Sweetie, but you'll soon have your own posters to put up and teddies to put on your bed."
Mandy looked up at Rose.

"But I've only got Katy," she said as she held up the doll she'd been carrying all this time.

"Well in that case she must have pride of place on your bed. Why don't you put her there while you have a bath?"
Mandy placed the doll on the bed, propping it up on the pillow.

"That's it. Come with me now and I'll run you a nice warm bath," said Rose as she went to the door and held it open for the little girl. They walked the few feet up to the bathroom door and entered. It was a large room; along the left hand side was a washbasin; above it a mirror stretched the length of the wall. On the right was a large white bath with a wood-effect melamine side panel. She reached over to a bathroom cabinet, which hung on the wall and took out a bottle of bubble bath then turned on the taps, pouring some of the peach coloured liquid under the stream of water that gushed out.

"There's nothing like a bath full of bubbles, I say," said Rose cheerfully as she screwed the cap back onto the bottle. "Let's get those clothes off and I'll leave you to have a lovely soak while I go and find a towel and some nightclothes for you to wear."

Rose helped the little girl to take off her dress and underwear, noticing that mark on her hand and various bruises all over her body. She also couldn't help but notice how thin Mandy was, her ribs protruding far more than they ought to. As well as this Rose noticed the smell of stale urine. She didn't say anything to Mandy; the poor girl had been through enough.

Rose put her hand in the water to test the temperature and to swish the bubbles around before turning off the taps.

"Here we are then. Are you ready?"
Mandy stood at the side of the bath looking worried.

"What's the matter Sweetie, don't you want a bath?"

"Is the water hot?"
Rose sensed the anxiety in Mandy's voice and realise that something was wrong. She put her hand in the water to show the little girl that it wasn't hot.

"It's just right. You can put your hand in first to make sure if you like."
Mandy held her own hand over the bubbles next to Rose's. Slowly she lowered the tips of her fingers into the water, thinking back to the horrors of the

scalding water from the last time she had a bath, and then the rest of her hand.

"Is it okay Sweetie?"

"Yes," answered Mandy as she pulled her hand out of the water.

"Put your arms up then, I'll lift you in." Mandy did as she was asked and lifted her arms above her head, letting Rose pick her up and place her gently into the warm bubbles.

"How does that feel?" asked Rose as she grabbed a flannel from the side of the bath and began softly washing Mandy's back.

"It's nice and warm," replied Mandy. The feeling of the water trickling down her back seemed to relax her. Rose washed the rest of Mandy's body then asked her to put her head back. Using a beaker, she gently poured water over the little girl's hair, careful not to get it into her eyes. Mandy closed her eyes while the old lady applied shampoo and gently rubbed it through her hair before rinsing it out again.

"Right, that's you nice and clean. I'm just popping out to fetch a clean towel and some nightclothes. I won't be a moment."

Rose left the bathroom, leaving Mandy on her own in the warm water. The little girl looked around. On the shelf above the basin were two multi-coloured beakers, each one with an assortment of toothbrushes and toothpaste. Two or three folded flannels, had been placed carefully over the edge of the basin. The bathroom was warm, the small radiator giving off plenty of heat.

Mandy looked down into the bath water and grabbed a handful of bubbles, covering her hand with the whit foam. She thought of Mummy and wondered what she was doing at the moment. Her thoughts were soon interrupted though, when Rose returned with a clean towel and a pair of pale-blue and white striped flannelette pyjamas.

"Here we are then. Are you ready to come put now?"

"Yes."

Rose held out the large towel while Mandy stood up. The old lady wrapped the towel tightly around her and lifted her out, placing her gently on the floor. Gently, Rose rubbed the little girl dry, took some talc from the cabinet and sprinkled it over her. Whilst rubbing in the powder, Mandy plucked up the courage to speak.

"Where are all the children?"

"At the moment they're in the dining room finishing their tea. After tea we have a quiet time, when we all go into the lounge and either watch television or maybe play a board game or two."

"Will I see them soon?" asked Mandy, keen to make friends with the children.

"As soon as you're dressed and have had something to eat I'll take you into the lounge and introduce you. Let's get these pyjamas on and then we can get going."

Rose helped Mandy to put on the pyjamas and pulled out the plug from the bath. She then folded the towel and hung it on a rail above the radiator. She turned towards the bathroom door and stopped in her tracks.

"Oh, how silly of me; I forgot your teeth!" she exclaimed, turning back around and heading for the wall cabinet. She took out a brand new toothbrush, tearing the packaging apart.

"There we are, a nice pink one just for you," said Rose as she handed the toothbrush for Mandy, "the toothpaste is by the sink."
Mandy found the toothpaste and put some on the brush, missing slightly and dropping some into the sink. She looked round, hoping that Rose hadn't seen her, fearing that she might get told off.

"Don't worry Sweetie, it'll wash off," said Rose, watching the little girl. Mandy finished cleaning her teeth and put the brush into one of the beakers with the others that were already there.

"Come on then, let's get you something to eat. You must be really hungry."
Mandy followed Rose out of the bathroom, back along the corridor and out of the doorway leading to the staircase. She held tightly to the bannister as she stepped carefully down each stair. Once they reached the bottom Rose led her through the doorway from which Jonathon Norris had come running out earlier. Mandy entered the large room and looked around. There were four rectangular tables, each with four chairs tucked under them. In the centre of each table were a cruet set and two bottles of sauce, one red and one brown. Each table had four cork placemats, with knives, forks and spoons set neatly around them.

There was an open door at the back of the dining room, from which the sound of crockery and cutlery being washed could be heard. Rose made her way into the kitchen closely followed by Mandy.

"Hello Sally," said Rose to the member of staff who was just finishing off the washing up, "is there any chance you could find something to eat for this young lady? She's had a long day and must be very hungry."

"Of course I can," replied Sally as she dried her wet hands on a tea towel. She walked towards Mandy and took her hand.

"Now what do you fancy? The other children have had their tea so you can choose anything you like."

"I don't know," answered Mandy shyly.

"Come with me to the fridge and we'll see what there is, shall we?" said Sally as she led the little girl to the most enormous refrigerator she had ever seen. Rose left the younger member of staff with Mandy in order to catch up with the other children who were by now in the lounge.

Sally was tall with short dark hair, shaped neatly at the neckline. She was twenty three and had wanted to work with children all her life. She had worked hard to become a care assistant, spending three years at university gaining the relevant qualifications and understanding of what was involved in this line of work.

"Do you like cheese Mandy?" she asked.

"Yes."

"How about cheese on toast then?"

"Okay."

Sally took a large portion of cheese and took it over to the worktop. She then opened the first of two breadbins and took out two slices of bread from an opened loaf. She lit the grill on an industrial-sized cooker and placed the slices evenly under the flame. She then took a sharp knife from the drawer and cut four slices from the block of cheese. While waiting for the toast to brown Sally spoke to Mandy.

"I expect this all feels a bit strange to you, but don't worry you'll soon get used to us."

"Will I be going back to Mummy soon?"

"We'll just have to see how things work out. Rose has told me a little about what's been happening and by the sound of it you need a little break from home," answered Sally, careful not to get Mandy's hopes up.

"But Mummy's all on her own," said Mandy with a worried look on her face.

"Mummy will be fine. Try not to worry." Mandy watched intently as Sally prepared the meal.

"Come and sit in the dining room," said Sally as she took the plate into the other room. Mandy followed and waited while Sally pulled out a chair at the nearest place setting.

"You can use your fingers if you like," said Sally as she cut the slices into quarters, "I'll just go and fetch you a drink. Do you like lemonade?"

"I love lemonade. Mummy used to buy it when I was little."

"Well there's always plenty here, Rose makes sure of that. Eat up and I'll go get some," replied Sally as she disappeared into the kitchen.

Mandy tucked into her meal, enjoying every mouthful. Sally didn't expect her to eat so much so was surprised when she returned to find half of it gone already.

"My, you are hungry! When's the last time you had a good meal then?"

"When I went to Nanny's, when Mummy didn't come to get me from school. Nanny made chips."

Sally couldn't believe what she had just heard. How could any mother not feed her child properly? She stood looking out of the leaded window into the dark night outside while Mandy finished her meal.

It wasn't long before Mandy had finished. Sally took her plate into the kitchen and came back through into the dining room.

"Right, I think Rose is waiting for you in the lounge with all the children. Are you ready to meet them?"

"Yes," answered Mandy, exited but also a little nervous. Sally took her hand and led her out of the dining room to the main hallway, then through a set of double doors into a corridor. As they walked along Sally pointed out the few doors along the way.

"This room here is the office," she explained at the first door on the right, "you'll usually find Rose in here doing paperwork."

The next two doors on the left were the girls' and boys' toilets. Opposite them was the staff room. Sally explained that this room was 'out of bounds' to any of the children except in an emergency. The last door leading from the corridor was the one now directly in front of them. Mandy could hear laughter and shouting from inside the room and began to tremble, nervous of meeting the children.

Sally turned the handle and opened the door. She led Mandy into the room and spotted Rose with a child on her lap, reading a story. As Mandy was led across the room towards Rose she looked around at all the children.

Susan and Ruth were sat on two armchairs, sharing a pop magazine. Joanna was also sat in a chair, reading a book she was studying for school. There was an argument going on in one corner of the floor; Luke and Jonathon, the thirteen year old twins had been playing marbles but one of them had accused the other of cheating. In the opposite corner was a large television, in front of which five children were engrossed in an adventure film.

Nobody had seemed to notice the new arrival until Rose spotted them.

"Ah, here you are," she said as she got out of her chair, leaving little Sophie to carry on with her book. She moved to the television and turned down the volume.

"What did you do that for?" groaned one of the boys who had been watching the film.

"I'll turn it back up in a minute, but first we must welcome our new guest to the house. Please say hello to Mandy."

"Not another girl!" groaned Luke, "why couldn't we have a boy?"

"'Cos boys are horrible," replied one of the girls.

"Now now, that's enough of that," ordered Rose as she introduced Mandy to each of the children in turn. She started with the five sat in front of the television.

"This is Anna," she said, pointing to a pretty blonde haired girl, "she's eight years old."

"Hello Mandy," said Anna politely.

"This is Sarah, she's Anna's sister and she's six years old."

"Hello," replied Sarah. She looked identical to her sister, the only difference being that Sarah wore glasses.

"And these three young men are Stephen, who's fourteen…"

"Hi Mandy."

"And Aaron, who's ten and David, who is six," continued Rose introducing the youngest boys.

"Why have you got your 'jama's on?" asked David inquisitively.

"Because she's just had a bath and it will soon be bedtime," interrupted Rose before Mandy had a chance to speak.

"Can you turn the telly up now please?" asked Anna.

"Okay, but it's bedtime for all you younger children when the film's finished," replied Rose as she looked around the room.

Luke and Jonathon were still arguing over their marbles; Susan and Ruth had carried on reading their magazines and Joanna continued studying her book.

"She can come and watch the film with us," offered Anna and Susan in unison.

"That's very kind if you girls, thank you," said Rose.

Mandy walked over to where the two girls had shuffled up on the floor in front of the television, leaving just enough space for her to sit.

"I'm just going to my office but I'll be back in about ten minutes when the film finishes. Please don't make too much noise, children," said Rose as she left the room.

Mandy sat quietly next to the girls who were engrossed in the film. After a couple of minutes she felt a tug on her hair. She ignored it but a couple of minutes later she felt another tug, this time a little harder. She looked around to find Aaron sat directly behind her.

"What are you looking at?" he asked, rudely. Mandy ignored him and turned back to watch the television. Suddenly she felt a sting as Aaron flicked the top of her ear.

"Ouch, stop it!" said Mandy, looking back at the boy.

"What?"

"Leave her alone, you bully," ordered Anna, punching Aaron in the shin.

"I'm not doing anything, she's telling lies!" The children carried on watching the film for a couple of minutes until the temptation became too much for Aaron and he flicked her ear again.

"Stop it!" demanded Mandy as she shuffled forward slightly to move away from the boy.

"Why, what you gonna do about it?"

"Just leave her alone Aaron," said Anna, "why don't you pick on someone your own size?"

"What, like you?" he replied, kicking Anna hard in the back.

Anna screamed before bursting into tears. Aaron laughed, proud of what he had just done.

"You're nothing but a bully. You only pick on girls 'cause you're too scared to pick on a boy," cried Anna, rubbing her back.

"I'm not scared of anybody, I only pick on you 'cause you're ugly!"

Anna suddenly forgot the pain in her back as she lunged at Aaron, pulling at his t-shirt and trying to drag him to the floor. The boy was too strong for her though, and he pushed her away, following her with a punch to her mouth. Anna wiped her mouth with the back of her hand and noticed the blood as she pulled it away. Just at that moment Rose walked back into the room.

"What on earth is going on in here?"

"It was Anna, she started it," shouted Aaron before anyone else could get a word in.

"He was picking on Mandy so I called him a bully and he hit me," said Anna, still wiping the blood from her mouth.

"Is this true Aaron?"

"She asked for it. I wasn't picking on anyone."

Rose turned to Mandy.

"Was Aaron picking on you?"

Mandy looked at the boy. He had a look in his eye, as if to say 'don't you dare say anything'. Then she looked at Anna; if she hadn't stuck up for Mandy then she wouldn't have that cut on her lip.

"Yes. He was pulling my hair and flicking my ear."

"Thank you Mandy," said Rose before turning back to the boy.

"Go to your room please Aaron. I think an early night might help to cool that temper of yours."

"But I didn't do anything. Why do I always get the blame?"

"To you room, now!" ordered Rose sternly.

"Okay I'm going," said Aaron as he stormed towards the door. As he opened it he turned back to Mandy.

"I'm gonna get you, new girl. You shouldn't have told on me."
The door slammed behind Aaron as he stormed out of the room.

"Don't worry about him," said Rose to Mandy who looked terrified. "He says things he doesn't mean when he's in a temper."

Rose looked at Anna's cut lip and gave her a piece of tissue from her pocket.

"It's not as bad as it looks, just a small graze. What have I told you about fighting with Aaron?"

"But he was picking on Mandy."

"Well you should have come to find a member of staff and let us deal with it. You know the rules, no fighting."

"I'm sorry Rose."

"That's ok. Anyway, the film's just finishing so it's bedtime for all you younger ones. Come on boys and girls."

The younger children, including Mandy, Anna and Sophie made their way out of the lounge and along the corridor towards the staircase. Anna and her sister caught up with Mandy as they walked.

"Don't take any notice of Aaron, he's a bully."

"Is your mouth okay," asked Mandy.

"Yeah its fine, I'll get him back tomorrow."

"How will you do that?"

"Not sure yet, but me and Sarah will think of something when we're in bed tonight. We'll tell you tomorrow."

"Okay," said Mandy. They walked the rest of the way in silence with Rose following behind.

Once they were by their bedroom Sarah and Anna said goodnight to Mandy, closing the door behind them. Rose then led Mandy and Sophie further along the corridor to their bedroom and opened the door. Sophie went straight for her pillow and lifted it to reveal her nightdress, which had been placed underneath it. While she was getting herself changed Rose pulled back the covers on Mandy's bed, carefully lifting Katy up and giving it to the little girl as she climbed into bed. Mandy held the doll tightly as Rose tucked her in and gave her a goodnight kiss.

"I'll see you in the morning Mandy. If you need the toilet it's the door almost opposite this room."

"Okay," replied Mandy as she turned onto her side, her back towards Sophie's bed.

Rose helped Sophie to get into bed and said goodnight to her before switching off the light and leaving the room, closing the door gently behind her.

It was suddenly very dark and quiet in the room. Mandy looked around, trying to make out shapes from the shadows. Through the drawn curtains she could see the moonlight shimmering, giving off just enough light for her to see around her. She turned to face the other bed in the room, noticing that Sophie had sat up in her bed.

"Mandy," whispered Sophie as quietly as she could.

"What?"

"Are you tired?"

"A bit."

Sophie climbed out of her bed and sat on the edge of Mandys. Mandy sat up, propping her pillow up against the headboard and then leaning back on it.

"So why are you living here now?"

"I don't know really. Some people came and said that I need a break from my Mummy."

"Oh," replied Sophie.

"Why are you here?" asked Mandy in return.

"My mum's in prison and there's no-one left to look after me."

"What about your Dad?"

"I haven't got a Dad."

"Nor have I," replied Mandy, "My Dad died."

"Oh."

"Why's your mum in prison?"

"Not sure, I think the police found some drugs or something in the house. My mum said they weren't hers but the police didn't believe her."

Mandy didn't really understand what drugs were but she didn't want Sophie to know that, so she went along with her as if she knew what she was talking about. Suddenly the two girls heard footsteps coming along the corridor. Sophie jumped down from Mandy's bed and into her own just as the door opened.

"I hope that wasn't you two I could hear talking," said Rose as she popped her head round the door.

"No Rose," answered Sophie.

"Okay, goodnight girls."

"Goodnight," replied the girls as Rose closed the door.

"Better go to sleep now, Rose gets really annoyed if we mess about at bedtime," warned Sophie.

"Okay," said Mandy as both girls snuggled up in their beds and closed their eyes. Within minutes they were both asleep.

Chapter 15

It was about 8 o'clock the following morning when Mandy was woken up by a cheerful voice.

"Come on, you sleepy-heads, time to get up!" said Rose.

Mandy opened her eyes and it took a few seconds before she remembered where she was. She sat up and looked around to see Sophie just getting out of her bed and putting on some clothes. Rose waked towards Mandy. She had some clothes in her hand; some underwear, a t-shirt, skirt and a jumper.

"Here, these will do you for now until your Social Worker takes you out to get some more clothes on Monday."

Mandy took the clothes and started to get dressed with Rose's help.

"Will I see Mummy today?"

"No. It may be a little while before you see Mummy, but don't worry, she'll be fine."

"But she's all on her own with no-one to talk to," said Mandy in a worried voice.

"I promise you Mummy is okay. Now off you go with Sophie to brush your teeth and have a wash. Then when you're both ready Sophie will take you down to the dining room for breakfast."

"Okay," replied Mandy as she and Sophie headed for the bathroom.

Once finished there, the two girls headed along the corridor towards the large staircase. As they reached the top of the stairs a voice called them from behind.

"Hey, wait for us!" shouted Sarah. She and Anna had just come out of their room and were also heading down to the dining room. Mandy and Sophie waited while the two girls caught up with them.

"Have you thought how you're going to get Aaron back yet?" asked Sophie.

"Yes, but we'll have to wait until it's our turn to set the breakfast table before we can do it," answered Sarah.

"What are you going to do?" asked Mandy.

"I can't tell you at the moment but it will be really funny 'cos everyone will be watching when it happens," laughed Sarah. The four girls made their way into the dining room where most of the other children had already started their breakfast.

"Good morning girls," said a happy voice. Sally appeared from the kitchen with a small rack of toast, which she placed on one of the tables. "Mandy, you're on the far table with Anna, Sarah and Aaron."

Mandy followed the girls to the table where Aaron was already sat.

"That's your chair," pointed Sarah as she showed Mandy the chair opposite Aaron. Mandy tried to pull the chair out from under the table but it seemed stuck. She pulled it again but it wouldn't budge.

"Aaron, leave her chair alone," ordered Sarah to the boy.

"What? I'm not doing anything. It's not my fault she's a little wimp who can't even move a chair."

"Just leave her alone, bully," replied Sarah.

Mandy pulled on the chair again. At first it was still stuck, but suddenly Aaron released his grip and the chair fell backwards, taking Mandy with it. She got up quickly, embarrassed because everyone had been watching. Sally raced over to make sure she was okay and helped her onto the chair.

"Aaron Philips, I don't know why you have to be so nasty to everyone," said the care worker.

"What? Why do I always get the blame?"

Sally ignored Aaron's question and poured Mandy a glass of orange juice from a large jug that had been placed on the table.

"At breakfast time you all choose which cereals you want from over there," explained Sally as she pointed to a large sideboard just outside the entrance to the kitchen. "If you want anything else, like grapefruit or toast then just ask one of us and we'll get it for you."

"Aaron always has grapefruit, don't you Aaron?" said Sarah, nudging him in the arm and sniggering.

"What's it to you, ugly?" he replied, nudging her back.

"Come on you two. Can't we have a single mealtime without you both having a go at each other?" Sally interrupted, giving them both a stern look.

Aaron carried on with his grapefruit while the girls went over to the sideboard, poured some cereal into their bowls and returning to their seats. Sally wandered around the room, making sure all the children had everything they needed before disappearing into the kitchen.

After a few minutes Aaron finished his grapefruit and put down his spoon. The rule was that the children had to sit quietly when they had finished and wait for the others on the table to finish. But Aaron could never be still or quiet for one minute. He sat back on his chair and stretched out his legs in front of him, his feet reaching underneath Mandy's chair. All of a sudden and without warning, Aaron pushed hard with his legs against Mandy's chair. The little girl was just about to take a mouthful of her cereal but it ended up spilling down the front of her jumper.

"That's for getting me sent to my room last night," said Aaron nastily.
Mandy ignored the boy and lent forward in her chair so that she could continue her breakfast. Aaron didn't like being ignored so he kicked Mandy's shin as hard as he could.

"Ow. Stop it," said Mandy as the tears welled up in her eyes.

"You're not gonna cry are you, new girl?"

Mandy tried as hard as she could not to let Aaron see that he had hurt her, but that kick really did hurt.

"Are you alright?" asked Anna, who was sat next to Mandy.

"Yes." replied Mandy, reaching down to rub her leg.

At that moment Sally reappeared from the kitchen and looked around.

"Everyone okay?" she asked, looking around the room.

"Don't even think about telling," muttered Aaron under his breath.

The children finished off their breakfast and waited for Sally to clear the tables.

"Right, it's Sunday so we all know what that means don't we?" she said in a loud voice.

"Chore day!" came the groans from around the room.

"Right, let's have a look at who's doing what today," said Sally as she walked over to where the sideboard was. On the wall above it was a large piece of paper with a rota drawn out on it. The room went silent as she read out the duties for each of the children.

"Washing up breakfast and setting the lunch table is Susan and Ruth's turn today."

"I hate washing up!" Ruth announced, folding her arms in disgust.

"Washing up lunch and setting the dinner table will be Steven and Luke."

"I did it last week!" protested Steven.

"Well you'll just have to do it this week too," replied Sally as she continued. "Washing up dinner things and setting breakfast for tomorrow will be Sarah and Anna."

"Good!" said Sarah with a wide grin on her face.

"Why is it good Sarah?" asked Sally, "you usually complain when you have to wash up."

"I like washing up now Miss."

"Okay, whatever you say," replied Sally as she carried on reading out various jobs for the other children to do. As she finished Aaron pointed out that Mandy didn't have a job to do.

"Well that's okay, we'll just have to wait until the rota's written out for next week and Mandy will be included in it then."

"That's not fair. Why should we all have jobs when she doesn't?" asked Aaron.

"She can help me and Anna with the washing up and setting breakfast tomorrow," suggested Sarah, hoping that Sally would agree.

"Yes okay then that's a good idea. I'll mark it on the rota," said Sally as she turned to add Mandy's name to the rota.

"I can't wait 'til tomorrow," grinned Sarah giving Mandy and Anna a knowing look. Aaron had no idea what the girls were planning.

"Right; those with jobs to do now can you please make a start. The rest of you can go to the lounge or your bedrooms for now; it's a wet day today so there won't be any playing outside today."

The children made their way out of the dining room and to their various rooms. Mandy remained with Sarah and Anna and followed them to the lounge. As they were walking Mandy was suddenly barged from behind.

"How's your leg?" laughed Aaron as he rushed past the girls.

"Don't worry Aaron, you just wait 'til tomorrow," shouted Anna to the boy.

"Oh I'm *so* scared," he replied as he ran off out of sight.

The three girls went into the lounge and settled down to watch the television. The rest of the day passed by fairly smoothly, with just the odd skirmish between the three girls and Aaron Philips. Once dinner had been eaten and the rest of the children had either gone up to have baths or into the lounge, Mandy, Sarah and Anna were left on their own to wash up the dishes and set the table for the following morning's breakfast. Sarah, being the eldest, washed while the other two dried. Mandy and Anna were still in suspense as to what Sarah had planned for revenge on Aaron. The last of the dishes were out away so all that was left to do now was set the breakfast table. Sarah took out some spoons from the cutlery drawer and gave them to Mandy to place on the tables. Then she took out two piles of cereal bowls, one for her to carry and one for her sister. Once the bowls and cutlery had been placed on the table the boxes of cereal were place on the sideboard ready for the morning.

"Right, now for our revenge," announced Sarah, "Anna, you keep a look out in case anyone comes and Mandy I need you to get me the sugar bowl from our table."

The two younger girls did as they were told, Anna held the door slightly ajar so that she could see out to where the large staircase was, while Mandy fetched the sugar bowl and took it to Sarah in the kitchen.

Sarah emptied out the sugar from the bowl into the sink and rinsed it away under the tap. Then she walked over to the store cupboard and took out a large container of salt. Carefully she carried it over to the bowl and poured some in.

"Why are you doing that?" asked Mandy.

"Well, Aaron always has grapefruit for breakfast with loads of sugar on it. So I thought it would be really funny to see his face when he gets a mouthful of salt instead!"

"Disgusting!" laughed Mandy as Sarah put away the salt container.

"Quick, someone's coming!" whispered Anna from the doorway.
Sarah quickly picked up the sugar bowl and placed it on the table just as Sally walked in the room to check on them.

"All done girls?" she asked as she headed for the kitchen.

"Yes Sally, we've just finished," replied Sarah innocently.

"And in record time too! I'll have to get you three to do the washing up more often."

The girls followed Sally out of the dining room, grinning to each other like Cheshire cats. It was time for their baths now so they made their way upstairs.

"Don't tell anyone about this, not even Sophie," whispered Sarah to Mandy.

"I won't," came the reply as the two sisters went into their bedroom and said goodnight to Mandy.

Mandy entered her own bedroom and sat on her bed, contemplating what she had just been up to with the sisters.

"It's going to be fun living here," she thought to herself.

Aftcr a couple of minutes Sophie came into the room after having her bath. Sally followed soon after, tucking Sophie into bed.

"You don't need a bath Mandy, you had one last night."

"Okay," answered Mandy as she put on her pyjamas with Sally's help.

"Are you settling in okay here at Whiteways?" asked Sally as she tucked the little girl into bed.

"Yes, I think I'm going to like it here."

"That's good. You won't see me in the morning as it's my day off tomorrow. Ron and Karen will be on duty for the next two days so I'll see you later in the week. Goodnight."

"Goodnight," replied Mandy, smiling to herself as she snuggled under the covers.

Sally switched off the light and closed the door behind her. Mandy looked in Sophie's direction but the other girl was laid still, not saying anything.

"Are you okay Sophie?"

"I don't want to talk about it," answered Sophie.

"Why, what's happened?"

"Nothing, I just miss my mum."

"Yeah, I miss mine too," Mandy sighed. With all the excitement that had just gone on Mandy had momentarily forgotten about Mummy. She suddenly felt guilty for not thinking about her. Both girls remained silent until they fell asleep.

It was a little earlier the next morning when Mandy and Sophie were woken up, about 7.30 this time. Karen, one of the care workers on duty introduced herself to Mandy. She had blonde shoulder length hair, flicked out at the sides and smothered in hairspray to keep it in place. She had a friendly face, with bright blue eye shadow. Mandy thought she looked a bit like a Barbie doll. Karen was in her early thirties, married with two young children of her own. She had worked at Whiteways for about five years and was one of the children's' favourite members of staff.

"Its school for you today Sophie," said Karen as she looked in the wardrobe and pulled out a white shirt from its hanger and handed it to the little girl. She helped Sophie with the rest of her uniform whilst talking to Mandy.

"And you are off out shopping today I hear. I wish I could come with you, I love shopping for clothes!"

"Will I be going to school after shopping?" asked Mandy as she looked at Sophie in her smart uniform.

"Not for a few days or so. We need to sort out what's happening with you before we decide when you're going back to school. Anyway, you can help me later when you get back from the shops. There's always something I need a hand with. Hurry up then you two, or you'll miss breakfast."

At that moment Mandy remembered what her, Sarah and Anna had set up in the dining room. Smiling to herself she put on the same clothes she had worn the previous evening and hurried to the bathroom to wash and clean her teeth. As she made her way down the corridor she could see the two sisters ahead of her so she ran to catch up with them.

"We thought you were already in the dining room," said Sarah, "come on, I don't want to miss this for anything."

The three girls hurried down the stairs. They arrived in the dining room to find they had beaten Aaron to it, which meant that all they had to do now was wait. It wasn't long before Aaron entered the room, and by the time he sat at the table the girls and most of the other children were already tucking into their food.

"Grapefruit again Aaron?" asked Karen cheerfully to the boy.

"Yeah," grumbled Aaron.

"Got out the wrong side of bed this morning, did we?" asked the care worker in response to his voice.

"No," he snapped back.

"Well can we have some manners then please?"

"Yes, PLEASE."

"That's better," said Karen as she disappeared into the kitchen and returned again a couple of minutes later with a grapefruit, already halved and in a bowl. She placed it in front of the boy, leaving her hand on the bowl until she heard a thank you.

"Thanks," muttered Aaron begrudgingly.

Karen walked away from the table to attend to some of the other children. As she did so Aaron picked up the sugar bowl and his spoon. He always put at least two spoonfuls on and today was no different. Sarah, Anna and Mandy watched, trying desperately not to laugh as he dug his spoon into the fruit ready to take his first mouthful. He scooped up a large portion and opened his mouth wide. As quick as the spoon went in Aaron spat out the food, standing up and knocking the chair over behind him.

Mandy and the two girls could hold back no longer. All at once they burst into hysterical laughter, tears streaming down their faces as they saw the look on Aaron's face.

"What are you laughing at?" asked Aaron in a fit of rage, still trying to spit out the taste of the salt.

"Nothing!" Sarah managed to spurt out before another wave of laughter overcame her.

At that moment Karen rushed over to see what all the commotion was. The three girls were still laughing uncontrollably, making Aaron's temper worse than ever.

"What on earth is going on here?" she asked.

"Someone's put salt in the sugar bowl," shouted Aaron. At that moment the whole room erupted into laughter, realising what had happened.

"It's not bloody funny," screamed Aaron as he stormed out of the room.

"Right, that's enough. All of you please calm down," ordered Karen as she picked up the chair that has been knocked down. "I don't suppose you three know anything about this?"

"No Miss," answered Anna, still trying to stifle her laughter.

"What about you Mandy, do you know anything?"

"No Miss," came her reply too.

"And what about you, Sarah?"

"No Miss," she replied as the three girls looked at each other and burst into laughter again.

"Right, that's it. Sarah and Anna, you can go straight to your room when you get back from school tonight and lose privileges until I find out which one of you is responsible. And Mandy, I will give you the benefit of doubt this time as you're new to us, but let this be a warning to you: we do not tolerate this kind of behaviour at Whiteways."

The three girls put their heads down as they were being told off. Mandy was a little frightened but the two sisters were still trying not to let Karen see how funny they thought it was.

Once breakfast was finished, all the children apart from Mandy got themselves ready for school. The first taxi that turned up was for Susan, Ruth, Joanna and Steven just after 8.30. They all went to the same secondary school about a mile and a half away. Luke and Jonathon were taken in a second taxi, while Anna, Sarah, David and Sophie were collected in a third and taken to the local primary school.

All that were left now were Mandy and Aaron. He was always collected about ten minutes after the others by a minibus from a school about five miles away, which catered for children with behavioural problems. Being left with Aaron made Mandy a little nervous. Karen had popped to the office foe something so they were alone in the hallway. It wasn't long before Aaron started.

"I'm gonna get you and Anna for what you did to me at breakfast."

"It wasn't me," pleaded Mandy.

"Don't lie. I saw you laughing at me."

"I wasn't."

"Yes you were," argued Aaron as he punched Mandy in the arm.

"Leave me alone," cried Mandy as she rubbed her arm where it had just been hit.

"What's the matter, Scaredy-cat? Not got your friends here to protect you?"

"I'm not scared of you," replied Mandy, putting on the bravest voice she could.

"Yes you are. Look, you're shaking."

"No I'm not."

"Scaredy-cat, Scaredy-cat!" teased Aaron as he poked Mandy in the chest and pushed her backwards.

Mandy plucked up enough courage to push him back, which enraged the ten-year-old. With all his might he pushed Mandy as hard as he could, causing her to fall backwards and hit the back of her head on the bottom of the staircase. She began to cry just as Karen appeared again from the office.

"What's going on?" asked the care-worker as she helped Mandy up.

"He pushed me," sobbed Mandy as she rubbed the back of her head.

"No I didn't, she fell," protested Aaron.

"Go and wait by the door for your bus, Aaron," ordered Karen, "you can't be left for more than two minutes without somebody getting hurt."

"Well she asked for it," he exclaimed as he kicked his schoolbag in the direction of the front door, following it before slumping himself against the wall with his arms folded.

Within a minute or so the sound of the minibus could be heard as it made its way up the drive, coming to a stop a few feet away from the front door.

"Come on Aaron, it's time to go," said Karen, still comforting Mandy.
Aaron picked up his bag and opened the door before looking back at the little girl.

"I'm gonna get you," he sneered, running out and slamming the door before anyone had a chance to say anything back. The minibus pulled away after a couple of minutes.

"Don't worry about him, Mandy. He always picks on new children, but he soon gets bored of it and leaves them alone," said Karen, "anyway we need to get you ready as Diane will be here soon to take you out."

Mandy went with the care-worker up to her bedroom to find her shoes and coat.

"You're going to need to buy some warm jumpers, it's going to get a lot colder in the next few weeks."

Mandy stood while Karen fastened the buttons on her coat.

207

"Will I be able to take my new clothes with me when I go back home to Mummy?"

"Of course you will, but I think it will be a while before that happens."

"But will I see her soon?"

"I don't know Darling, it's not up to me to say. Why don't you talk to Diane when you're out today?" replied Karen. It was always difficult when children in care were so young; they didn't understand about all the various meetings, case-conferences and sometimes even court cases that were involved. All Mandy knew was that Mummy wasn't allowed to look after her at the moment.

Once Mandy had her coat and shoes on she followed Karen back downstairs.

"You can help me in the dining room if you like, while you're waiting?"

"Okay," the little girl agreed. She spent the next ten minutes or so collecting dirty cutlery and crockery from the tables and handing them to Karen to wash up. As the clock on the wall approach 10 o'clock the front doorbell began to chime. It was loud enough to be heard from the dining room, so Karen dried her hands with the tea-towel.

"Come on then, young lady. It's probably Diane here to take you out."

Mandy followed her out of the dining room and into the hallway.

"Good morning Mandy," greeted the Social Worker with a warm smile.

"Hello," replied Mandy, smiling back, pleased to see her familiar friendly face.

"Are you ready then? I'm glad you've got a warm coat on, it's a bit nippy out there," said Diane, rubbing her hands together in an effort to keep them warm.

"Yes I'm ready."

They said goodbye to Karen and stepped out into the cold. Diane opened the passenger side door of her car and held it against the wind while Mandy climbed in. She then walked around to her own side.

"Would you like some music on?" she asked after starting the engine.

"Okay."

Diane turned the dial on the car radio. The distinctive voice of Karen Carpenter filled the air. Neither the Social Worker nor Mandy spoke while the song played. Once the song was finished and the DJ started chatting Diane began to talk.

"Do you listen to music, Mandy?"

"No, not really; Daddy had lots of records which he used to play but Mummy hasn't played them since he died."

"That's a shame. There's nothing like a good song to keep you going."

Diane carried on driving, but instead of talking they both listened to the next two or three song that played. Mandy watched and listened to Diane as she hummed and recited the words of each one. She seemed to know every word off by heart. Soon they arrived at Bournemouth town centre and found a parking space. The two of them got out of the car, the strong wind blowing in their hair as they walked briskly to the first department store. Once inside, the Social Worker led Mandy up to the children's' department where they picked a couple of jumpers and some trousers.

Mandy felt as ease with Diane; it was as if they had known each other much longer than the two days since they had met. They paid for the clothes at the first store and spent the next couple of hours looking in different shops around the town, buying all the essential clothing that Mandy needed. Soon Diane had more bags than she could carry, joking to Mandy that her arms would drop off if they bought any more.

Once they had finished shopping they both decided they would get a bite to eat before going home, so they took all the bags back to the car and returned to find a coffee shop.

"How about a doughnut, I'm having one?" asked the Social Worker as she picked up a tray to put their food on.

"Yes please, my tummy's rumbling where I'm so hungry."

The Social Worker picked up two doughnuts and ordered a glass of cola for Mandy and a coffee for herself. Once the food was paid for they found a table and sat down to eat.

"So, how are you finding it at Whiteways? I bet it all feels a bit strange to you at the moment, doesn't it? Asked Diane as she picked up her coffee cup.

"It's okay."

"Just okay, have you made any friends yet?"

"Anna and Sarah are nice, but there's a boy called Aaron who's nasty to everyone."

210

"Yes, I know Aaron. Don't be too hard on him though Mandy, he's been through a very tough time and has a few problems."

"Okay," replied Mandy, taking a bite from her doughnut.

"I bet you can't eat that without getting sugar all round your mouth!" laughed Diane.

"Yes I can, you just watch," replied Mandy licking away the sugar that had already collected on her lips.

"Go on then," dared the Social Worker with a somewhat mischievous smile.

"Only if you do."

"Oh, so you want a challenge do you?"

"Yeah," answered Mandy with a sugary grin.

"Right then," said Diane as she picked up her own doughnut, "after three. One…two…three…"

At the same time they both opened their mouths as wide as they could, trying carefully not to let their cakes touch the sides as they put them in. Mandy took a bite but it was too late; a mixture of jam and sugar came spurting out all over her chin, dropping to the front of her coat. Without thinking, Mandy wiped her chin with the back of her hand, spreading the mess even further.

Diane managed to avoid the jammy part of her doughnut, but it hadn't stopped her mouth too being covered in sugar. They both looked at each other and laughed, causing the people around them to look and see what all the noise was about. Diane picked up a paper serviette and wiped the sugar

211

from her mouth before picking up another and cleaning Mandy up as best she could.

"See, I said you couldn't do it," laughed the Social Worker as she wiped away the last of the jam.

The two of them sat with their drinks when a woman with a small boy sat at the table next to them. The boy couldn't have been any older than Mandy and the woman the same age as her own mother. Mandy watched as the woman placed a bowl of chocolate ice cream in front of the boy. His little face beamed as he picked up his spoon and began tucking in.

"My Mummy used to buy me ice cream," said Mandy to Diane. The Social Worker sensed the change in Mandy's tone as she remembered her Mummy. She decided that now might be a good time to explain what was going to happen in the near future. She took a deep breath.

Mandy, Darling, I expect you're wondering what's going to happen now that you're at Whiteways."

"I'm just here until Mummy gets better aren't I?"

"Well, yes, in a way. The thing is, Mummy needs quite a lot of help at the moment and no one really knows how long that will take. I will be talking to her tomorrow to see how she is and to set up a meeting between her and some other people to see just what we need to do to help her."

"Will she be able to come and see me?"

"That is one of the things that will be talked about at the meeting. Hopefully within a few weeks

212

something can be arranged. I will let you know everything that happens but please don't worry, Mandy. Everyone is working to do what's best for you and your Mummy."

"Okay. So does that mean I will be at Whiteways for a long time?"

"I honestly don't know Darling. These things can sometimes be sorted quickly but other times it takes a bit longer. Anyway, I think it's time we got back now, they will be wondering where you are."

The two of them left the coffee shop and headed back through the cold wind to the car. Almost without thinking Diane turned on the radio. Slade were blasting out one of their glam rock hits and it wasn't long before they were both singing at the tops of their voices all the way back to Whiteways. The Social Worker seemed to have a knack of cheering Mandy up without even trying. It was as if they were sisters or best friends, despite the age difference or the official connection between them.

Once home, Mandy showed off her new clothes to Karen and Rose, who had come back on duty.

"I'm sorry about all the jam on Mandy's coat," laughed Diane, "we had a bit of a competition and ended up in a right mess."

"That's okay, there's not much a washing machine can't sort out," replied Rose, "it's just good to see that Mandy's enjoyed herself."

Diane said goodbye to Mandy and promised she would see her in a few days after the meeting with her mother. Mandy, with the help of Rose, took all her new clothes to her bedroom to put away.

"So you had a good time then?" asked Rose as she placed some of the new underwear in a top drawer.

"Yes. I like Diane, she's really nice"

"I've got some good news for you Mandy. We've decided that you should get back to school as soon as possible."

"But what about my uniform, it's still at home?" asked Mandy worriedly.

"That's okay, I've got spare uniform in the store cupboard from children that have lived here in the past who have gone to you school."

"Can I go tomorrow then?"

"Yes if you want to, although I thought you might want to leave it a few days before you went back."

"No, I miss my friends."

"Well that's settled then, tomorrow it is. You'll need to have a bath tonight then."

"Okay."

Rose finished putting the clothes away and they both went back downstairs. It wasn't long before the other children were back home and the usual Whiteways chaos had begun again. Teatime came and went without too much arguing between Aaron, Anna and Mandy, although he made it quite clear that they hadn't got away with the 'grapefruit' incident. Soon it was time for Mandy's bath and bed. She was so excited about going back to school that she found it difficult getting to sleep.

"Good morning Mandy, it's lovely to see you again," greeted Mrs Albright as the little girl walked into the classroom. Immediately the teacher could see how much healthier and cleaner Mandy looked. She had been told about the Social Services' visit and the move to Whiteways. Mandy settled quickly back into the school routine; her two best friends Rachel and Shelley were also pleased to see her again and it wasn't long before she told them all about the events of the previous week.

Soon enough the whole class knew about Mandy and she became very popular, with everyone wanting to be her new best friend. There were one or two older children, however, who came to hear about Mandy and took it upon themselves to tease her about the fact she now lived in a home.

"Your Mummy didn't want you, that's why they took you away," sneered one boy.

"You live in that looney home for stupid kids, don't you?" said another one day in the playground.

Although the comments upset Mandy, she didn't let it show in public. Instead she seemed to develop a kind of barrier, which made her appear unaffected by any nastiness towards her. Even at Whiteways when Aaron had a go at her, or pushed or hit her for no reason she seemed to act as if it didn't matter to her.

Chapter 16

It was now just over a week since Ruby had said goodbye to her daughter. Since then she had been in a permanent drunken state, spending all her time on the sofa, getting up only to fill her glass or go to the toilet, although sometimes she didn't get as far as the bathroom. She had not washed nor bothered to brush her hair, or even get dressed. Why should she? There was nothing and no one to make an effort for anymore. All that was left now was alcohol; at least that went some way towards blocking out what was left of her life. Occasionally Ruby thought about Mandy; what was she doing now? Had she made many friends? Where was she? Up to now Ruby had heard nothing from Social Services; she still had no idea where they had taken Mandy and what was going to happen to her.

Ruby sat up on the sofa, where she had spent yet another drunken night. She looked over to the clock on the mantelpiece to see the time. 10.35. She stood up slowly and made her way out of the room to make herself some coffee. As she walked through the hallway Ruby spotted the pile of mail that had been dropped through the letterbox in the last few days. The throbbing in her head became almost unbearable as she bent down to pick up the letters. She stood straight again, rubbing her forehead with her free hand. As she walked into the kitchen Ruby sifted quickly through the mail, discarding anything which looked like junk onto the table. She was left with two envelopes and opened the first. It was from the council, warning her that she was now one step closer to being evicted for non-payment of rent.

"Why can't they give me a break," Ruby said to herself as she slammed down the letter and looked at the last remaining envelope. As she pulled the letter out she noticed the official headed notepaper of Dorset Social Services. She quickly pulled the letter out and began to read:

"Dear Mrs Croft,

Further to recent events, a meeting has been arranged between yourself and our department. Please attend our office (address above) on Tuesday 25th October at 1.30pm. It is important that you are able to attend, so if for any reason you can't be there please telephone so that another meeting can be arranged.

Yours Sincerely

Mr M Lawrence"

Ruby looked at the calendar on the wall and scanned through the days until it suddenly dawned on her that it was today.

"Shit!" she shouted as she looked at the clock. She had just less than three hours to sort herself out and get to that meeting. She took the kettle and filled it with water to make a coffee. vodka or anything alcoholic would have been preferable, but Ruby knew there was no way that she could be seen to be drunk today. She quickly drank her coffee and went upstairs for a bath. While the water ran, Ruby found some reasonably smart clothes in her wardrobe. She then sat on the edge of her bed for a moment, her head pounding.

217

"Come on, pull yourself together," she said to herself as she got up and made her way to the bathroom. Ruby laid back in the bath and closed her eyes. She thought about Mandy and realised that she was really missing her daughter. She also began to realise that whatever she said or did today would have a huge impact over whether or not there was any chance of Mandy ever coming back home.

After a fairly long soak, Ruby got herself dressed and for the first time in months she styled her hair and put on some make up. She managed to make herself look quite presentable, hiding the dark circles under her eyes and the pale, drawn complexion of her face. Over the past few months Ruby must have aged ten years; she was still, after all, only thirty-three.

At about 12.30 Ruby left the house. She had decided to walk the couple of miles to the Social Services office; she thought the fresh October air would clear her head and she needed time to think about what she was going to say to convince them that she was fit to look after Mandy. Ruby didn't seem to have acknowledged to herself that she had a serious alcohol addiction and there was no way that she was in a position to look after her five-year-old daughter.

Once outside the huge building that housed the Social Services department Ruby stood and lit a cigarette. She had about ten minutes spare to gather her thoughts before the meeting. She entered the building and made her way to the reception area, from where she was given directions to a room on the first floor. As she neared the room Ruby could feel the butterflies inside her; she felt like a naughty schoolgirl about to be punished by the head teacher. The door was open so she walked in slowly to find Mr Lawrence and Diane already sat at a large oval table, along with four other people, only one of whom Ruby recognised, that was Mrs Wade, the school head.

"Hello Mrs Croft, glad you could make it," greeted Mr Lawrence.

"Hello," replied Ruby, suddenly feeling very angry towards the Social Worker.

She pulled out a vacant chair from around the table and sat down. She was desperate for a drink to get her through the next hour or so, but knew she was going to have to try her hardest not to think about it.

"I think we're all ready now," said a man sat opposite Ruby. The others all nodded in agreement as he spoke again.

"I think the best way to start is for everyone to introduce themselves in turn so that we all know who's who and what role we have at this meeting. I'll start with myself. My name is Roger Lamb and I am a Team Leader for the Social Services. I oversee any decisions that Mr Lawrence or Diane Parkes make, although I don't get as involved with individual families as they do."

He looked to his left, prompting the woman sat next to him to speak.

"My name is Dr. Mason and I'm a child psychologist."

Ruby looked at Dr. Mason with contempt. What the hell did she know about bringing up

219

Mandy? She probably had no kids of her own, learnt everything out of a text book.

The next to speak was Diane Parkes, who quickly explained that she was Mandy's appointed Social Worker, but would be assisted by her colleague Mr Lawrence. Next was Mrs Wade, then Ruby herself. She didn't speak when prompted. Why should she? Everyone knew who she was.

"We all know Mrs Croft, Mandy's mother," said Roger Lamb. Ruby just stared straight ahead, avoiding eye contact with anybody. They quickly moved on to Rose, who explained that she was Officer-in-Charge at Whiteways children's home.

"So that's where she is," uttered Ruby under her breath.

"Okay, now that we are all acquainted I think we can get started. We all know that the reason we are here is to decide what is best for Mandy," began Mr Lamb, "I've read through the reports and it seems there are issues that need to be addressed with regard to Mrs Croft and whether or not she is able to look after Mandy at this point in time."

Ruby remained silent. She suddenly felt really angry as she felt everybody looking at her. She really wanted to tell them all to leave her and Mandy alone to get on with their lives, but knew all she could do was sit and listen to her future being decided for her.

"Miss Parkes, you have visited Mrs Croft and Mandy at home, what is your view?" asked Mr Lamb.

220

"Mandy and her mum have had a lot to deal with in the last year, with death of Mr Croft. I think this has been especially difficult for Mrs Croft, having to suddenly bring up a young child on her own."

"When you say difficult, what do you mean?"

"Well the evidence seems to show that Mrs Croft has a problem with alcohol, which in turn is leading to Mandy being neglected."

"Neglected? No way!" interrupted Ruby, "What the hell gives you the right to judge the way I look after Mandy?"

"Please calm down Mrs Croft, shouting won't get us anywhere. You will have an opportunity to speak in a moment," said Mr Lamb. He turned to Mrs Wade.

"Mrs Wade, you have been watching Mandy closely over the past few months at school, what are you views?"

"Mandy has become very quiet at school, preferring to be alone rather than playing with her friends. This is totally different to when she first started at school, when she was always smiling and running around. Another thing we've noticed is the marks and bruises on Mandy's body. She always seems to be reluctant to explain how they came about."

Ruby could stay silent no longer.

"I hope you're not accusing me of harming my child. That's the last thing I'd do. You lot don't know anything."

"Mrs Croft," replied Mr Lamb, "we are not accusing you of anything. We have to look at everything in order to establish what happens next, and when we see a child with an excess amount of marks and bruises we have to be cautious."

"It still seems like you're accusing me," replied Ruby as she sat back in her chair and folded her arms, "all I want to do is get my daughter back."

"That is our aim too, Mrs Croft. We don't like to keep families apart any longer than is necessary. Our aim is to help you and Mandy get back on track so that in the end she can come back to you."

Ruby didn't reply, instead she nodded and looked straight ahead. Mr Lamb turned towards the Child Psychologist.

"Dr. Mason, in your experience what is your opinion of what you've heard?"

"From what I hear, Mandy was a very happy, easy to look after child. It seems that Mrs Croft has taken her husband's death badly and has used alcohol as a way of coping. Unfortunately this has had a negative effect on the way she has been able to look after Mandy. I feel that in order to bring things back to the way they were Mrs Croft needs to address her alcohol addiction, and until that is under control I think its best that Mandy remains at Whiteways."

"Thank you Dr. Mason," said Mr Lamb. He turned towards Ruby.

"Mrs Croft, you've heard what these people have had to say. Do you have anything you would like to add?".

Ruby had heard what everyone had to say and realised that she was going to have to work hard to get Mandy back. She sat up and took a deep breath before speaking.

"Things haven't been easy for me since my husband died. I've tried to do my best but everything is just so hard. I'm not an alcoholic but I do like to have a drink, it helps me cope. All I want is to have Mandy back home with me."

"Thank you," said Mr Lamb. He paused for a while before speaking again. "I feel that for the time being Mandy would be better off staying where she is at Whiteways. It will give Mrs Croft a chance to get back on her feet. I am going to appoint a counsellor to visit Mrs Croft and help her with her drinking problem. If this goes well then we can review in a couple of months to see if maybe there is a way that Mandy can go back home. Is everyone in agreement?"

Everyone around the table nodded except for Ruby.

"So does that mean I can't see Mandy?"

Mr Lamb turned to Diane Parkes for his next question.

"Miss Parkes, do you think it would be wise for Mandy to see her mother at this time?"

"I've spent quite a bit of time with Mandy over the last couple of weeks and I do know that she is really missing her mum. I think it would put both her and her mum's minds at ease to know that they are both okay. Maybe Mrs Croft could visit on a two-weekly basis."

"Okay," replied Roger Lamb turning to Ruby, "How about we start with an hour supervised visit every other Saturday at Whiteways?"

"Why supervised, can't I take her out for an hour?"

"I think under the circumstances supervised visits would be better, and then if all goes well after a few weeks then maybe you will be able to take Mandy out."

"Looks like that's the best I'm gonna get, I suppose I should be grateful that you will let me see her at all."

"Okay, that's settled then," said Mr Lamb as he concluded the meeting.
Arrangements were made for Ruby to visit Mandy at 2 o'clock the following Saturday.

Once the meeting was over Ruby made her way out of the building. She now realised it wasn't going to be at all easy to get Mandy back. For a start she would have to give up the drinking. That was going to be harder than anything. A counsellor was going to visit and try to help but unless Ruby herself was determined to give up then what was the point? Ruby started to walk home, thinking about what had been said at the meeting. She made a conscious decision on her way home: from today she was giving up the vodka. All she had to do was think positive and of having Mandy back home. It couldn't be that difficult, could it?

Once home, Ruby sat in the kitchen and looked around. Empty vodka bottles, cigarette packets, and overflowing ashtrays. The contents of the bin spilled out onto the floor and the sink was full of dirty crockery. She walked into the lounge where she was greeted with a similar picture; empty glasses, full ashtrays, and a dirty blanket thrown down on the sofa. Ruby dared to go upstairs; she opened Mandy's bedroom door and looked in. The stench of stale urine was still as strong as ever. She closed the door and went back downstairs to the kitchen. There she took the full bag from the bin, taking it outside to the dustbin. On her way back indoors Ruby spotted Mandy's bike in the middle of the garden. She burst into tears as she headed back indoors and sat at the table, sobbing.

"What have I done? I'm so sorry Mandy, I'll make it up to you I promise," Ruby said to herself as she cried.

After a strong cup of coffee Ruby got up and worked throughout the rest of the afternoon and into the evening, throwing out all the rubbish, vacuuming the lounge carpet and washing up all the dirty dishes. By the time she had finished Ruby was exhausted. She really needed a drink but was more determined than ever to keep her promise to herself. Instead she made some coffee, which she took up to bed with her. Before long she fell asleep whilst thinking about her daughter and looking forward to seeing her on the following Saturday.

Chapter 17

On Saturday morning Mandy woke up early, excited about seeing Mummy for the first time since moving to Whiteways. 2 o'clock seemed to take forever to come around, but when it finally did Mandy was waiting by the front door. The bell rang and Mandy jumped up and down with excitement as she waited for Rose to open the door.

"Mummy, Mummy!" she shouted as she jumped to give her mum a big hug.

"Hello sweetie. Oh, I've missed you so much," said Ruby as she held her arms tightly around her daughter.

"If you would like to follow me there's a room we can use where we won't be disturbed," Rose interrupted. She led Ruby and Mandy along the corridor into a small room. There was a table and four chairs in the room and along one wall was a small bookcase with a selection of children's' books and a few board games.

"I'll just get on with some paperwork," said Rose, sitting herself at the table and opening a file which she had been holding.

Ruby pulled a chair away from the table and sat down.

"Come and give Mummy a hug," she said, holding her arms out. She lifted Mandy onto her lap and kissed her gently on her forehead.

"So, what have you been up to sweetie? Have you made any friends here?"

"Yes Mummy. Anna and Sarah are my best friends. They're really nice."

"That's good. So are they looking after you properly here?" asked Ruby, glancing over to Rose.

"Yes, and we have really big dinners here, and nobody's allowed to leave the table until it's all eaten up."

"That's good then. Hopefully you won't get too used to it here or you won't want to come back home to me."

"Yes I will Mummy, when can I come back?"

Ruby looked towards Rose, unsure of what she should be saying to Mandy. Rose put down her pen and turned to Mandy.

"We are all working towards getting you back home to Mummy, but it will take some time before that happens. In the meantime Mummy will still be able to visit."

"Okay," said Mandy, sounding a little disappointed.

"Don't be sad sweetie," said Ruby, "I'm doing my best to get myself sorted out and I'm sure it won't be long before you can come home."

It seemed like no time before an hour had elapsed and it was time for Ruby to leave.

"Can't you stay a bit longer Mummy?" asked Mandy, tugging at her mum's arm.

"I really wish I could sweetie, but we have to do as the Social Worker says. I promise I'll be back in two weeks to see you."

"But I don't want you to be on your own," said Mandy as she began to cry.

Ruby knelt down to hug her daughter, her own eyes filling with tears.

"I'll be fine, please don't worry about me. You just make sure you have fun and be good."

"I will Mummy."

Rose opened the door, indicating that Ruby really should be going. She followed as Ruby and her daughter walked to the front door hand in hand.

"Goodbye sweetie," said Ruby, trying her hardest not to cry.

"Bye Mummy," replied Mandy as Rose put her hand on her shoulder. She stood and watched as Ruby blew a kiss, and gently closed the door behind her.

"Why don't you go and find Anna, I think she's in the lounge?"

"Can I go to my room, I don't want to play?"

"Of course Darling," said Rose as she watched Mandy make her way to her bedroom.

Mandy was quiet for the rest of the day, spending most of it on her own in her room. Over the next few days, Anna and Sarah managed to cheer her up; she had settled in well into life at Whiteways, getting on well with all the children apart from Aaron. She tried to avoid him as much as possible, although mealtimes were difficult as she still had to sit opposite him.

Diane Parkes came to see Mandy soon after Ruby's first visit, to see how Mandy and her mum had got on.

"I like seeing Mummy," Mandy explained, "but I'm sad that she's at home on her own."

228

"I'm sure Mummy is fine. She knows all this is to help you and her in the long run and she is trying very hard to stop drinking so you can go back to her."

Little did Diane know that Ruby was really struggling to cope since seeing Mandy. It broke her heart to walk away and leave her at Whiteways. Ruby found herself in a horrible catch 22 situation. She knew the only way to get Mandy back was to stop drinking, but the only way she could cope with Mandy not being there was to drink.

The more Ruby drank to get herself through the day, the more she hated herself for not being strong enough to stop. She had a five-year-old daughter who longed to be back home and she didn't even have the determination to get herself sorted. The Social Services had left numbers for Alcoholics Anonymous and other supports groups, but Ruby had just put them to one side, still denying to herself that she had a big problem.

Ruby was also getting to the stage where she couldn't afford the vodka that kept her going, and a couple of days after her visit to Mandy she found herself in the supermarket, desperate for a drink. She walked to the wines and spirits section where she picked up a bottle of vodka. Looking around, Ruby quickly hid the bottle under her jacket. She looked around again, no-one had seen. Quickly she made her way through the store towards the checkouts, fearing that she had been spotted and that maybe they were just waiting for her to walk out of the store. Ruby trembled as she walked through the checkout area, smiling at a cashier as she passed. She walked out of the store, quickening her pace as she stepped out onto the street. After about twenty yards she paused and looked behind her. She breathed a sigh of relief as she realised she had got away with it, and then walked around the corner, spotting a bench.

As she sat down, Ruby pulled the bottle from under her jacket. She unscrewed the cap and took a large swig. A middle-aged man walked past her, giving her a disgusted look before muttering something under his breath.

"What's you problem?" Ruby sneered as she took another swig, but the man just ignored her and walked away. She was beginning to feel the cold by now so tucked the bottle back under her jacket, supporting it with one arm, and began to walk back home. As she walked though, Ruby began to feel ashamed of what she had done. How had things got so bad that she was now stealing alcohol just to get through the day?

Once home, Ruby immediately poured a glass from the bottle. She went into the lounge and spent the rest of the day drinking and sleeping. The next week or so until her next visit to Mandy were spent much the same way.

Saturday came and Mandy was as excited as ever. 2 o'clock came and once again she was waiting by the front door. She waited five minutes, no sign of Mummy. Another five minutes and still no sign. Mandy began to think that Mummy had forgotten her but she still waited. After a further ten minutes, which to Mandy felt like an eternity, the doorbell rang.

"I'm so sorry," slurred Ruby as Rose opened the door, "the bus was late."

"Mandy was getting awfully worried, she thought you weren't coming." replied Rose, smelling the alcohol on Ruby's breath. "Never mind, you're here now."

Mandy took her mum's hand and they walked through to the same room as before. Ruby almost lost balance as she pulled out a chair from under the table.

"Oh, silly me," she said, trying to make a joke. Rose gave a stern look, which Ruby took offence to.

"Oh dear, looks like we're not amused today," she said, turning towards Mandy. "So what have you been up to then sweetie?"

"Nothing really," said Mandy, sensing that Mummy was in a strange mood. She knew the signs too well; the slurred words, the sarcasm. Mandy knew that with one wrong word Mummy could change at any moment.

"Nothing? Well great place this is then isn't it? What do they do, leave you shut in your rooms all day?"

"No Mummy, we get to play games and watch TV."

"You could do that at home with me."

Rose could no longer sit and say nothing.

"Mrs Croft, please remember that you are here to see your daughter, not to criticise the way we do things here at Whiteways."

"Oh I'm so sorry," said Ruby sarcastically. She looked back at Mandy. "Looks like I've got to watch what I say or I'll get told off by Miss Bossy-boots."

Rose ignored the comment but said to herself that one more word out of turn then Ruby would have to leave. Ruby managed to refrain from upsetting Mandy for the rest of the hour.

"I'm afraid it's time for you to leave now, Mrs Croft," said Rose as she looked at her watch.

"Can't I stay a few minutes more?" asked Ruby.

"I'm afraid not. I've already extended the time as you were twenty minutes late and I'm not allowed to extend visiting times without prior notice."

"Rules, rules, I'm sure you could give us just ten more minutes." said Ruby who was getting agitated.

"I'm sorry Mrs Croft. It's time for you to leave and that's that. Now please say goodbye to Mandy."

Ruby stood up a little too quickly and felt dizzy. She sat back on the chair.

"Are you okay Mummy?" asked Mandy.

"Yes I'm fine sweetie; I just got up a bit quick. Come and give me a hug then I have to go. I'd better do as I'm told or I won't be allowed to come back and see you."

Mandy gave her mum a hug and walked with her to the front door. They said goodbye and Ruby shut the door behind her, completely ignoring Rose.

"Are you okay Mandy?" the care worker asked.

"Yes. I think Mummy was in one of her bad moods."

"I think so too," said Rose, putting her arm around the little girl, "why don't you go and find the others, I think they're watching a film?"

"Okay," replied Mandy as she walked slowly from the hallway.

Rose looked on, feeling sorry for Mandy. All the excitement of seeing her mother was wiped out with just a few nasty comments. Ruby could go home and blot out the world with a drink or two, but a child takes everything to heart. All Rose could do was be there to pick up the pieces.

It took Mandy a few days to get back to her normal self, but was soon looking forward to seeing Mummy again. Soon enough the next visiting day came around and Mandy waited patiently by the front door. Only this time she waited and waited. From 2 o'clock till 3 she watched through the window but there was no sign. Rose could do nothing but watch as Mandy waited in vain. She tried to persuade her to wait in the lounge with the other children but Mandy refused.

"Mummy will be here, she promised."

By 4 o'clock Mandy was still waiting. Rose put her hand on the little girl's shoulder.

"Mandy Darling, I don't think Mummy's coming."

Mandy turned to Rose and burst into tears.
"Mummy doesn't love me anymore."

"Oh Darling, Mummy does love you but she has lots of problems at the moment."

"No she doesn't, if she did she would be here now."

Mandy ran from Rose up to her bedroom and threw herself onto her bed, crying inconsolably. Rose followed but all she could do was sit on the edge of the bed and watch as Mandy cried and cried.

Many cried herself to sleep that evening and when she got up the next day she spoke to no-one. Rose and Karen both tried but Mandy said nothing. Anna and Sarah did their best but Mandy wouldn't even come down for breakfast. If Mummy didn't love her anymore then what was the point? She just stayed on her bed, refusing to move.

An hour or so later there was a knock on the bedroom door. Mandy ignored it but looked round to see Diane enter the room.

"Mandy," said the Social Worker as she sat at the edge of the bed close to the little girl.

Mandy sat up and put her arms tightly around Diane's neck, bursting into tears again as she explained that Mummy didn't love her anymore.

"Oh Darling, I'm so sorry that Mummy let you down. I know you don't understand but Mummy has problems that will take a long time to sort out. She doesn't mean to hurt you but she doesn't know that she's doing it."

"But if Mummy doesn't love me anymore what will happen to me?"

234

"Mummy does love you, but at the moment she doesn't know how to cope. She needs to sort herself out, but until she does you know that Rose and the other staff are here for you, and you know you can call me any time you want to."

"If Mummy can't look after me, can you?" asked Mandy as she released her grip slightly and looked up at Diane.

The Social Worker felt that overwhelming compassion again; at that moment she would have loved to have taken Mandy home with her, but knew circumstances would never allow it.

"Oh Darling, I wish I could but I'm not allowed to. I will do all I can to help you and Mummy though, but you must promise me that you will be strong and look after yourself by eating properly. I would hate for you to make yourself ill. Anna and Sarah are very worried about you too, they like having you to play with."

"Okay, I will," said Mandy as she gave Diane another hug, "will Mummy come and see me soon, do you think?"

"I'm sure that will happen, but I think it will probably be a little while before you see Mummy again; she needs a bit longer to get herself well again."

"Okay."

Diane helped Mandy to dress and walked down to the dining room with her for breakfast before leaving. For the rest of the day though, she couldn't stop thinking about Mandy. Although there were many children in similar circumstances to Mandy she seemed to have struck a chord with her.

Sometimes it was difficult to separate her job from her personal life.

Ruby had finished the stolen bottle of vodka in no time that evening and drunk herself to sleep. In the morning she was desperate for another and soon found herself on a mission to find some more 'free' alcohol. She put on her long winter coat, it wouldn't look suspicious in the cold weather, but the best thing about it was the large pockets, including one on the inside. It was ideal for what Ruby had in mind. She made her way to the supermarket, heading straight for the wines and spirit section. She looked around before quickly picking up two small bottles of vodka, slipping them into her inside pocket. The adrenaline was pumping inside her as she made her way out of the store. Ruby was almost enjoying her new-found excitement; once again she walked about twenty yards up the street before stopping to look back. She had done it again, it was easy.

Ruby walked home, grinning to herself as she did so. She was pleased with herself but now wanted more, so instead of going in and drinking she put the bottle on the side and headed straight out again. This time she thought she'd try a different supermarket, so she walked in a different direction until she came across another shop. Once again she found the drinks section and looked around. This shop was a little busier so she would have to be careful. As she slipped the bottle into her inside pocket Ruby realised an old man at the other end of the aisle had spotted her.

"Hey!" he shouted, causing other shoppers to look round.

Ruby panicked and ran, knocking into a trolley with a young child in it.

"Watch it!" shouted the young mother as she comforted the crying child.

Ruby ran towards the checkouts as fast as she could, pushing through the queue of shoppers waiting there. She ran straight out of the store, still clutching the bottle in her pocket close to her, not looking back but running as fast as she could until she was at least two hundred yards away. She paused to catch her breath, leaning back against a wall and looking back to see if she was being chased. She had got away with it again. Ruby laughed as she made her way home.

With her newly discovered talent for stealing, Ruby now had an endless supply of vodka. The addiction was out of control and she was now permanently drunk, existing by way of the bits of food that she managed to steal along with the alcohol. She looked a mess; not bothering to wash or to change her clothes, the house stunk of the mixture of stale nicotine, alcohol and body odour. Apart from the odd outing to top her supply, Ruby lived in her lounge, spending most of her time semi-conscious on the sofa.

A few days after failing to turn up to see Mandy, Ruby received a letter from the Social Services. She poured herself a drink before reading it.

Dear Mrs Croft,

In light of recent events, we have decided that it is in the best interest of your daughter Mandy that you no longer have supervised visitation with her. If circumstances change we will review the situation, but until that time please do not attempt to contact Mandy.

Ruby gulped down the remainder of her drink and threw the glass against the wall, smashing it to pieces.

"Bastards!" she shouted out loud, "They can't stop me seeing my own daughter."

She found herself a new glass and poured another vodka before returning to the sofa, where she remained for the rest of the day, trying not to think of Social Services because when she did it made her angry.

The next day Ruby began to realise the reality of what the letter meant; this time though, instead of getting angry she began to think about how she had managed to get herself and Mandy into this situation. Why did she treat Mandy so badly? What had that poor girl done to deserve being placed into care? Ruby cried; there was no way now that she would ever get Mandy back no matter how she tried. The drink had taken a hold and there was no escape.

Over the next few weeks Ruby became more and more depressed. She couldn't even bring herself to move from the sofa and spent all her time drinking, sleeping and crying.

Mandy became very withdrawn over the next few weeks, only speaking when spoken to and not joining in with any activities with the other children. Diane was extremely worried and visited Mandy almost every day. Even at school Mandy was quiet and on a few occasions Mrs Albright found her sat on her own, crying. No one could really get through to Mandy; the only person able to get a few words out of her was Diane.

A week before the end of term Mandy was sat alone on a bench in the playground. She began to think about Mummy and how she wanted to be there for Christmas, which wasn't far away. She looked towards the school gate and recognised the person standing there. It was Mummy. Mandy ran over as fast as she could.

"Mummy, what are you doing here?"

"Hello sweetie, I just had to see you."

From across the playground Mrs Albright spotted the two of them at the gate and began to walk over. Ruby saw her and knew she had to be quick.

"Listen Mandy, meet by after school by the corner shop. You can come home for tea."

"But I'm not allowed to, we'll get into trouble."

"Don't worry, I'll sort it. Please don't tell anyone, it's our little secret, will you do that?"

At that moment Mrs Albright reached the gate. She took Mandy's hand and began to lead her away.

"Mrs Croft, this is not a good idea. Will you please leave or I will have to call the police."

"I'm sorry; it won't happen again, I was just passing." She turned to Mandy. "Bye sweetie, see you soon."

Mandy walked away with the teacher, smiling to herself. She was going to see Mummy. Ruby made her way back home, praying that Mandy would meet her; this was going to be a special night.

The afternoon went slowly for Mandy. She was both excited and nervous. Somehow she would have to walk out of school without being seen by anyone. A taxi would be waiting for her so it wouldn't be long before they would be looking for her.

The end of day bell rang and Mandy's heart began racing. She was first out of the class, running down the corridor and out of the main door, joining a group of children so as not to be spotted. She mingled with them as they walked out of the main gate and into the street where parents were waiting. Looking back to make sure no-one had spotted her, Mandy ran as fast as she could towards the corner shop. As promised, Ruby was there to meet her daughter, her arms held out to give her a big hug.

"Oh Mandy, I was so worried you wouldn't come. I've missed you so much."

"I've missed you too Mummy," replied Mandy as she put her little arms around her mum.

"Come on, we'd better get home quick," said Ruby as she held Mandy's hand and led her down the street towards home.

Meanwhile at school, Mrs Albright looked out of the window and saw the taxi waiting outside the school entrance.

"That's funny," she thought to herself as she looked at her watch, "the bell went twenty minutes ago."

She walked out to where the driver was waiting.

"Who are you waiting for?"

"Little Mandy, the one who goes to Whiteways. It's not like her to not be here when I come, I thought maybe she's got sports or something."

"No, she should be here. I saw her leave the classroom, she was first out. I don't know where she could have got to…oh no, her mum."

Mrs Albright suddenly remembered seeing Ruby and Mandy at the gate at lunchtime. She told the driver to go and rushed back to the office to alert Mrs Wade. After one last search of the school Mrs Wade rang Rose at Whiteways to make sure Mandy hadn't walked home by herself, but there was no sign of her. Rose phoned Diane Parkes at once.

"I'll go straight round to Mrs Croft's house. If Mandy's anywhere then that's where she'll be. I'll call the police too.

"How does Spaghetti Bolognese sound? I went shopping especially this morning; I know it's your favourite."

"Yummy, yes please!"

"That's settled then, come and sit in the kitchen with me while I get it started. You can tell me all about school and how you're getting on."

Ruby and Mandy chatted away while dinner was cooking, both of them relaxed and cheerful, forgetting recent events and being a normal mother and daughter once again. Ruby knew it was only a matter of time before there would be a knock at the door and she would have to say goodbye to Mandy, so she did her best to make her as happy as possible in the short time they had together. They ate dinner and then played some of the board games that Mandy still had at her mum's house.

Then came the inevitable knock on the door.

"It's time for you to go back now Mandy sweetie," said Ruby as she stood to answer the door.

"But I want to stay Mummy. Please don't let them take me away again."

The door knocked again, this time a little harder.

"I'm sorry Mandy, you have to go. There's nothing I can do about it," replied Ruby, tears in her eyes.

She held on to Mandy's hand as they walked towards the front door.

"Please Mummy, no," Mandy pleaded as the letterbox opened and Diane Parkes peered through.

"Mrs Croft, please open the door," she said in a calm voice.

Ruby turned to Mandy and knelt down to her level.

"sweetie, this is hurting me as much as it is you and I am so sorry, but you have to go with the

242

Social Worker. You know I love you, don't you sweetie?

"Yes Mummy, and I love you but why can't I stay?"

"It's just the way it has to be, I'm so sorry sweetie," sobbed Ruby as she rose up and opened the front door.

Diane Parkes stood alone at the door, but Ruby could see two police officers at the front gate, ready to enter if needed.

"I'm sorry Mandy but I have to take you back to Whiteways. You really shouldn't be here with Mummy and she could get into a lot of trouble for bringing you here."

"Please don't tell Mummy off, she only wanted to see me. She didn't do anything wrong," said the little girl as she clung to her mum.

"It's okay Mandy," said Ruby, "Miss Parkes is right, I shouldn't have brought you here. You really do have to go back to Whiteways now; promise me you'll be a good girl sweetie. You will be alright, I promise."

"But what about you, Mummy? You'll be all alone again. Who will look after you?" cried Mandy as Diane took hold of her hand.

"I'll be fine; now off you go with Diane. Don't forget to tell them you've had dinner."

The Social Worker led Mandy out of the house towards the front gate. It was dark outside and getting very cold.

"Bye Mummy, I love you," sobbed Mandy, tears streaming down her little face.

"Bye sweetie," replied Ruby as she blew a kiss to her daughter and watched her walk down the path. Diane Parkes turned back to Ruby and spoke.

"You know we'll be in touch about this Mrs Croft. Please don't try anything like this again or you will be arrested."

"Don't worry, it will never happen again; please promise you will take good care of Mandy, she's all I have in the world."

"I promise she'll be taken good care of, Mrs Croft," replied Diane as she walked out of sight with Mandy.

Once back at Whiteways Rose gave Mandy a bath and settled her into bed.

"Goodnight Darling, try to get some sleep. You must be tired after your adventure today," she said as she gave Mandy a kiss on the forehead.

"Will Mummy get into trouble now?" asked the little girl.

"I don't know what will happen with your Mummy, but she will need to understand that she can't just take you from school when she feels like it. You must also let me or your teachers know if you see Mummy again Mandy. That is really important."

"Okay. I'm sorry but Mummy said she was missing me and I just wanted to see her again."

"Don't worry Darling, you're back here and you're safe; that's the most important thing of all. Get a good night's sleep and we'll say no more about it," said Rose as she tucked Mandy in and switched off the light.

"Goodnight Rose."

Alone again, Ruby felt the emptiness of the house. She poured herself a drink and sat at the kitchen table, looking around at the appalling state of the room. How had her life become such a mess? Two years ago life was so different; with Derek and Mandy she was happier than she could ever have asked to be. Why had she been dealt such a bitter blow? How did she get to the state of being unfit to look after her own daughter?

Ruby could no longer stand it. With the help of half a bottle of vodka she decided that for her own sake and Mandy's she was going to end it all. Mandy was better off without a drunk for a mother, she thought to herself. 'When she's older she will understand that I didn't mean to hurt her, and hopefully she will understand why I did what I'm about to do.'

Ruby found an old notepad on the kitchen table and a pen nearby. She tore a page from the book and began to write.

To my beautiful daughter,

I hope you enjoyed having dinner with me today and that you didn't get into trouble. I was so pleased to see you again. Mandy I need to tell you how sorry I am for everything. I never ever meant for you to get hurt. Please remember that I love you very, very much and always will. I truly hope that you have a wonderful life and that all you wish for comes true.

Goodbye my sweetie,
Love Mummy.

245

By the time she had finished writing, Ruby was sobbing her heart out. She read the tearstained note and folded it in half and wrote Mandy's name on the outside before leaving it on the table. She stood up and reached for a high cupboard door. Standing on tiptoes she grabbed a plastic box containing a variety of tablets and medicines. Ruby placed the box on the table and took out two plastic bottles of aspirin and a handful of other tablets in blister packs. With the tablets and opened bottle of vodka, she made her way upstairs to her bedroom where she sat on the edge of her bed. She placed the bottle on the bedside table and slowly pushed out all the tablets from their blister packs and emptied the two bottles of aspirin onto the bed.

One by one, Ruby started to put the tablets into her mouth, each followed by a swig of vodka. Then she scooped a few up into her hand and pushed those into her mouth. With the help of the vodka she managed to swallow all the tablets, ignoring the acrid taste in her mouth and trying not to gag as they became stuck in her throat. She then picked up the vodka bottle and drank the remainder in one go.

Ruby felt sick; her vision was blurring and all she could do was lay on the bed. As she did so, blackness came over her and she closed her eyes to the world. Ruby never woke again.

Chapter 18

The weekend at Whiteways was a busy one for the children; they were all getting excited because it was time to make the Christmas decorations. Rose and Sally had gone up into the attic and found last year's cards and showed the children how to make them into lovely hanging ornaments. They also made paper-chains out of strips of coloured crepe paper, all competing to see who could make the longest.

Mandy did her best to join in but was worried about her mum. She sensed that something was wrong but didn't know what.

"Come and help us Mandy," called Anna, "We're gonna make the longest paper-chain in the world."

"Okay then," said Mandy as she joined the girls.

"What's wrong Mandy, you're not very happy today are you?" asked Anna.

"She's never happy, she's just a girlie cry-baby," Aaron butted in.

"Leave me alone. Why do you always pick on me?" asked Mandy.

"Because you're stupid and I feel like it," retorted Aaron as he threw a piece of screwed up paper at her.

Mandy felt so alone. Here she was in a room full of people she didn't really know and just about to spend her first Christmas away from Mummy. What had she done wrong to be made to live in a home? Was she really so naughty that Mummy couldn't cope with her?

Soon enough Monday morning came around, and the start of another school week; it was the last week before the Christmas holidays. At the end of the day Mandy went to the office as usual to wait for her taxi to arrive, but was surprised to find Diane Parkes waiting for her.

"Why are you here?" she asked as she smiled at the Social Worker.

"Hello Mandy, I've come to take you out; there's something I need to tell you."

"What is it?" she asked excitedly. "Can I go back and live with Mummy?"

"Oh my Darling, no that's not it. Let's go for a drive and I can tell you then."

Diane led Mandy to her car and they drove to a quiet spot overlooking Bournemouth bay. It was a cold, bright afternoon, the sun just beginning to lower and create a beautiful orange glow across the water.

"So what is it then?" asked the little girl as the car came to a stop.
Diane switched off the engine and turned towards Mandy. This was going to be the hardest thing she had ever done as a social worker.

"Mandy Darling, I've some very bad news to tell you."
Mandy looked worried, she knew it was going to be about Mummy.

"I'm not allowed to go back home and live with Mummy, am I?" she asked.

248

"I'm afraid it's not that," said Diane as she took hold of Mandy's hand, "there's no easy way to say this, but Mummy died on Friday night."

"But I saw Mummy on Friday. That was the day I went home for tea after school. She was okay when I left her." Little Mandy couldn't believe what she was hearing.

Diane clasped both her hands over Mandy's and spoke softly, struggling to hold back the tears.

"I'm afraid it's true. Mummy fell asleep and didn't wake up again. I'm so sorry Mandy."

"It was that drink she has wasn't it? I should have been home to look after her, it's my fault."

"Mandy it's not your fault, you couldn't have done anything to help Mummy. She left a note after you left on Friday to tell you how much she loved you and how sorry she was for everything she put you through.

Mandy felt sick. Her whole world had been taken from her. First Daddy and now Mummy.

"Are you okay Mandy?" asked Diane, "do you want to go for a walk or anything?"
Mandy didn't answer, she just sat in silence. After a few minutes she turned to Diane.

"Can I go back now?"

"Yes of course, are you okay Mandy?"

"Just take me back."
The social worker started the engine and began the drive back to Whiteways. She wanted Mandy to speak, but she said nothing all the way back to the Children's' home.

As the car came to a stop Mandy opened the door of the car and walked straight in through the front door of Whiteways, not waiting for Diane, who followed as quickly as she could. Rose rushed towards the door as she heard it open but Mandy ignored her, walking quickly through the hall and up the stairs to her bedroom.

Later that evening Rose tried to console Mandy but she was devastated and eventually cried herself to sleep. No one could get through to Mandy; not even Sarah nor Anna could comfort her. It became a struggle for Rose or any of the staff to get Mandy to come downstairs for meals, and when she did she didn't speak to anyone. The only person that could get anywhere with her was Diane. She seemed to have a way of talking to Mandy and getting her to explain her feelings and fears of what would happen now that she had no one.

Soon it was time for all the children at Whiteways to get involved in preparations for Christmas. They all tried to include Mandy, even Aaron who had shown surprising concern for Mandy, but she just didn't have the heart to join in. Christmas Day soon came around but to Mandy it was just another lonely day. Without Mummy there was no point in having fun anymore. She joined in with the unwrapping of presents but was just going through the motions, not really taking notice of what her presents were and who they were from. Nanny and Granfy had sent her gifts but they reminded her of Mummy too much and she became upset.

Later in the day, once everyone had settled in the lounge, Aaron sat down next to Mandy.

"I have a present for you," he said as he handed her with a small box.

Mandy took the box and opened it. Inside was a dainty silver bracelet with a heart-shaped charm attached to it.

"It was my Mum's. She gave it to me before she died."

"I didn't know your Mum died too," said Mandy as she picked the bracelet from its box.

"I don't talk about it, but I thought you should know that I know what it's like."

"Thanks Aaron, but I thought you didn't like me."

"Most people think I'm horrible but I can't help it, it's just the way I am since Mum died and I ended up in this place. I just seem to be angry all the time because they don't understand what it's like not to have your Mum around."

"I understand. It's horrible and I don't know what to do. Will I feel sad forever?"

"No you won't, but you have to try as best you can to get back to normal and start playing with your friends again."

"But I don't feel like I have any friends."

"You've got me, I will help you to feel better."

"Thanks Aaron."

Chapter 19

Within a few weeks and with Aaron's support Mandy began to feel better. Life at Whiteways continued and soon Mandy began to pick up some of Aaron's mischievous ways. He was still angry towards most people but he and Mandy developed a bond and looked out for each other. On one occasion after a row with Rose, Aaron persuaded Mandy to run away with him. Although apprehensive, Mandy saw it as an adventure and agreed, so they gathered up what pocket money they had between them and crept out of the back door and across the large field and through a gap in the hedge.

"Where are we going to sleep?" asked Mandy, worried at the thought of spending a night under a bush.

"We aren't far from Poole Quay, I thought we could sleep in one of the boats there. No one will ever find us there."

"I think we should go back home Aaron. I've never run away before and we will get into trouble."

"Don't be silly. I'll look after you, and anyway Rose doesn't care about us, she just gets paid to look after us."

"Okay, but I'm scared," said Mandy as she reluctantly followed Aaron who seemed to know where he was heading.

Dusk was just setting in as Aaron led Mandy into a boatyard on the quayside. He looked around at all the boats that had been taken out of the water for repairs and renovations.

"How about this one?" he asked as he pointed to a small white boat with a blue hull and covered cabin.

"I don't know Aaron, I want to go home. It's getting dark and I'm cold."

"Come on, let's look inside," said Aaron as he clambered up the side of the hull up onto the small deck.

He held his hands out for Mandy to grab and she made her way onto the boat.

"Let's see what's inside," said Aaron as he walked around to the door leading to the small lower compartment. The door opened easily.

"Come on," he called back to Mandy, "it looks okay in here, there's enough room for us to sleep in here."

Mandy followed Aaron down the small steps that led into the hull. She looked around, it was dark but she could still make out a small cushioned bench along one side.

"So what do you think?" asked Aaron. "No one will find us here and we will be safe."

"I don't like it, I want to go home."

"We can't go home now, it's dark outside and it's starting to rain. We will be okay in here, I promise. Look, I've got some food."

Aaron undid his rucksack and rummaged until he pulled out a packet of biscuits and some sweets. He opened the packet and gave a biscuit to Mandy.

"See, I said I'd look after you didn't I?"

"Yes, thanks," replied Mandy as she sat on the bench. "I suppose one night will be okay."

The two children sat and ate most of the biscuits and talked about life at Whiteways and how they both ended up there. Mandy felt safe with Aaron; although not too much older than her he seemed to have a maturity about him; which was so different from the way he acted in front of the staff and social workers at the home. As it got later the rain outside became heavier and the wind gustier, whistling through the boatyard and shaking the boat they were in. Mandy was scared, she began to cry so Aaron laid down next to her on the bench and they huddled together, listening to the elements outside. Eventually tiredness overcame them and they fell asleep.

Mandy was woken early the next morning by Aaron shaking her.

"Come on, we've got to go, the boat people will be here soon and we can't let them see us."

"What?" asked Mandy as she realised where she was.

"We've got to go before they spot us." Said Aaron as he carefully opened the cabin door and looked out. It had stopped raining but was cold and misty by the waterfront.

Mandy followed Aaron out and carefully they climbed down from the boat and out of the yard before they were spotted.

"So what do you want to do now?" asked Aaron, keen to carry on their adventure.

"I want to go home. I'm cold and hungry."

Aaron was disappointed but he could see that Mandy wasn't happy and knew he had to do the right thing.

"Okay, I'll take you home then," he said as they started to walk back in the direction of home.

"Will we be in lots of trouble?" asked Mandy on the way back.

"Probably, but they are never cross for long, I've done it before loads of times."

"I don't like getting into trouble."

"You'll be okay, it's the first time you've done anything like this so it won't be too bad."

Soon enough they were back at the driveway leading to Whiteways. They hadn't even reached the front door when it flew open and Rose ran out towards them.

"Thank God you're safe, both of you. What on earth were you thinking Aaron? Do you not realise how old Mandy is? We've had the police out searching for you both."

"I'm sorry," said Aaron, "I looked after her though.

"That's not the point, get inside and I'll deal with you in a minute."

Aaron did as he was told and headed inside. Rose turned to Mandy, who was terrified at what was going to happen now.

"Are you okay Mandy? What on earth made you run away like that? Did Aaron make you go with him?"

"No he didn't, I wanted to go."

"Well don't you ever do anything like this again, do you hear?"

255

"I won't, I'm sorry." Replied Mandy as she began to cry.

"Come on, let's get you in and into some dry clothes. I need to ring the police and Diane Parkes to let them know you're home safe.

It wasn't long before the incident was forgotten and Mandy settled back into the routine of life at Whiteways once again. She and Aaron remained good friends and apart from when they were at school they were inseparable. Soon it was spring and the children were able to play outside more and more. One day they were out playing French cricket when Aaron got called in by Rose. He came back out again but Mandy noticed he wasn't happy.

"What's wrong Aaron?"

"I've got to leave."

"What do you mean?"

"The social services have found a foster family for me to stay with. They want me to go as soon as possible."

"That's good isn't it?" said Mandy, trying to put on a brave face for Aaron's sake. She always thought Aaron would be with her at Whiteways and was going to miss him.

"It is I suppose, but it means I might not see you again and you're my best friend."

"I know, I will miss you too."

It wasn't long until it was time for Aaron to leave. Mandy was heartbroken as she wave goodbye to him, she felt so alone again, just like the time when she found out Mummy had died. Diane did all she could to try to cheer Mandy up but nothing really helped until she bought her a small cassette player and some music tapes for her to play. The music really helped Mandy through her bad days, and she spent hours on her own in her room listening to anything and everything she could get hold of. On Sunday evenings the top 40 was played in the radio, and Mandy recorded it all every week.

It was decided by social services that Mandy should be adopted as she had no family capable of looking after her. Diane explained to her that it would be a slow process and so she would be at Whiteways for quite a while longer.

Chapter 20

Once a year at Whiteways all the children went on a camping holiday, so in July 1976 they all travelled by minibus to Glastonbury. The children had a wonderful time swimming, playing crazy-golf, racing along an assault course. On one of the warm evenings they all went for a walk up to the tower on the top of Glastonbury hill. As they looked down there was a fairground a short distance away. Mandy was awestruck; the beautiful, magical sunset across the hills in the distance and the lights of the fairground down below were like nothing on earth she had ever seen in her young life. She sat on the ground, the noise of the other children faded as she thought of Mummy and how she would have loved her to be here right now.

Mandy's train of thought was interrupted by Rose, who had sat down next to her and put her arm around her.

"It's beautiful, isn't it?"

"Yes, it's like magic. Can we go down to the fair?"

"Of course, that's what I came to say. We are heading down there now. Are you coming?"

Mandy stood up and held Rose's hand as they and the rest of the group made their way down the hill towards the fairground. Mandy had the time of her life, she had never been to a fairground before. The music and lights of the rides amazed her; the magnificent painted horses of the carousel, the hook-a-duck stool, the coconut shy. It was too much for her to take in and the evening went far too quickly before it was time to walk the short distance back to the campsite, all holding huge candyflosses and cuddly toys which they had won.

Once back home Mandy couldn't wait to tell Diane all about her holiday.

"It was amazing, there was a huge funfair and I went on all the rides. You should have seen it, there was a magical sunset. I wish I could go back there."

"Well maybe one day you will. It's always nice to have a special place that you remember."

"I want to go back there when I have a proper family again."

I'm sure that will happen Mandy. Anyway I have some news of my own to tell you." said Diane.

"What is it?"

"I'm getting married next year."

"Really? That's good. I've never been to a wedding before."

"Well there's one thing I wanted to ask you, Mandy."

"Yes?" asked Mandy excitedly.

"How would you like to be my bridesmaid?"

"Really?"

"Yes, I can't think of anyone else I'd rather have than you."

"Yes please!" Mandy jumped up with excitement and threw her arms around Diane.

"That's settled then. I will come back and see you soon and we can arrange a time to go out and choose your dress.

Mandy could hardly wait as the day of the wedding drew near. She had been out with Diane and had chosen a beautiful flowing turquoise dress with matching shoes and tiara. Soon enough the big day arrived, and Mandy couldn't have been prouder as she followed Diane down the aisle to meet Richard, her new husband to be. It was a day to remember, and Diane and Richard thanked Mandy for making their day so special.

Soon enough though, Mandy had to go back to Whiteways and hope that soon someone would be able to adopt her. Months went by but no progress seemed to be being made. In the summer of 1977 a big Silver Jubilee party was arranged in the New Forest for hundreds of underprivileged children. Everyone from Whiteways was there, all the staff and even Diane. The children had a fantastic time, with food and games all afternoon.

Mandy noticed that Diane was looking sad. It was unusual as she was always so cheerful.

"What's wrong Diane?"

"Oh, it's nothing really, I've had some bad news that's all."

"Please tell me, I've always told you all my problems haven't I?" said Mandy sounding very grown up.

"Yes that's true but it's not really something that I should tell you Mandy as you're so young."

"Please tell me, I don't like it when you're sad."

"Okay. It's just that I've been told by my doctor that I can't have children of my own."

Mandy put her little hand in Diane's and turned to her.

"Why don't I be your little girl?" she suggested innocently.

"You can't Mandy. I'm your social worker and wouldn't be allowed to." said Diane, taken aback slightly by the suggestion.

"That's a shame," said Mandy, "I would love to come and live with you."

"It's a really lovely thought Mandy, and if things were different I would have loved it too. Anyway, I'll always be your friend even when you've left Whiteways and have a proper family to look after you."

But Diane couldn't dismiss the thought of somehow being able to look after Mandy on a permanent basis. She talked it over with Richard and he was more than happy with the idea of adopting Mandy. Diane made enquiries and began the process of adoption, although she kept it quiet from Mandy in case of disappointment. Finally, after months of talks and meetings Diane and Richard got the go ahead they so badly wanted.

Throughout the following autumn and winter months Mandy became accustomed to life at Whiteways, feeling that she would be there forever as no-one apart from Diane ever came to visit her. She often wondered why Nanny and Granfy never came but never did find out why. Through the spring Diane took Mandy out on trips to the park and the New Forest. Mandy felt loved and wanted when she was with Diane, and often asked her to adopt her. But Diane still kept quiet, the excitement brimming and the wish to tell Mandy almost unbearable until she knew for definite that Mandy could be their adopted daughter.

Finally, in June 1978, just before Mandy's tenth birthday Diane was able to give Mandy the news she had waited for.

"Hi Diane! I'm going to be ten tomorrow!"

"Double figures eh? You're growing up too quickly!" said Diane as she gave Mandy a hug at the door of Whiteways.

"Have you got me a present?" asked Mandy excitedly.

"It's not your birthday until tomorrow, but I have something I need to talk to about Mandy. Let's go and sit in Rose's office."

"What is it?" asked Mandy as they sat down at the table.

"I'm afraid I won't be able to be your Social Worker anymore."

"Why not? I don't want a new Social Worker."

"Because I'm leaving my job to look after a very special little girl."

"Oh," said Mandy, her head bowing down to the floor.

"Her name is Mandy and I'm going to adopt her."

Mandy suddenly realised what Diane had just said.

"Me? You're allowed to adopt me?"

"Yes, you. You can come and live with me and Richard."

"Yippee!" shouted Mandy as she jumped up and gave Diane the biggest hug, tears of happiness streaming down her little face.

Epilogue

The warm late summer sunset was beautiful. As the three figures reached the tower at the top of Glastonbury Hill they sat and watched the majestic sunset lower into the horizon, orange and purple lighting up the sky as far as they could see.

"I love this place, it's magical."

"Do you remember me telling you that you would come back here some day with a proper family?"

"Yes I remember, and I secretly wished it would be you with me."

"So did I."

Mandy smiled to herself as she sat looking at the sunset. Either side of her, each with an arm around her were Richard and Diane, her new family.

265

11496778R00148

Printed in Great Britain
by Amazon.co.uk, Ltd.,
Marston Gate.